# A DAMNED DIRTY THING

## THE JAKE BISHOP FILES
## DOC BLALOCK

EDGE WEAVER LLC

**A Damned Dirty Thing**
**The Jake Bishop Files**

Edge Weaver Realms is an imprint of Edge Weaver LLC

Book Design: Marie Ito

Kindle ISBN: 978-1-968100-20-9

Paperback ISBN: 978-1-968100-21-6

Published in the United States of America

Edge Weaver LLC
19360 Rinaldi #681
Porter Ranch, CA 91326-1607

# DEDICATION

For Tacy, my raison d'être. Special thanks to Anthony Romano, Patrick Sealy, and Marie Ito for their valuable help, support and guidance.

# CONTENTS

# ACT I: THE HUNT BEGINS

It's been ten long months since the blast that tore through my life, leaving only pain and ashes in its wake. They said it wasn't my fault, nothing I coulda done, but the guilt sits on my shoulders like a lead weight.

Frank Donovan, my partner and friend, vanished in the smoke and flames that engulfed our office. They never found his body. Our secretary, Mary Parker, was killed too. Quiet funerals for friends that I could not attend.

My recovery was a slow crawl through the wreckage of shattered bones and flash-burned skin. The surgeries, the opiate highs, and finally, the detox from the drugs and their artificial solace were behind me.

Now, here I am, back on the rain-sodden streets that echo with memories. Irongate, my little piece of Solomon City, sprawls out in front of me, a landscape of towering buildings and dark alleyways where secrets linger in the shadows.

My name's Jake Bishop, private investigator.

Bailey's Diner, a neon-bedecked refuge in this urban jungle, beckons with the promise of hot coffee and cool quiet, a welcome respite from the miserable rain. The waitress, an old soul in a young face with eyes that have seen too much, greets me.

"Hiya Bishop," she says, as if routine can bring back what's lost. "Anything to eat?"

"Just coffee," I reply. "Waiting on someone."

The familiar booth, the warm light, and hot coffee soothe me as I watch rivulets of rain run down the window, obscuring the skyline. Memories flicker—Frank's laughter, the hum of the city outside our office window, and then the blinding light of the explosion. It's all there, etched in the lines on my face and the ache in my bones. I flinch involuntarily at the memory.

Recovery, they call it. But some wounds never truly heal. The window reflects a man I barely recognize, a man who's tasted the darkness and come back changed.

Frank and I had been running a routine case. Bail jumper. Pretty big bounty on him. Neither of us knew the kid was connected. It just never twigged. Turns out, his aunt is married to a boss in the Italian outfit. Morelli. Vito Morelli. We were working late that night. Our secretary had rolled up her sleeves to work right alongside. Apparently, we'd gotten a little too close. Morelli had bombed the office. Somehow, I survived. I awoke in the street staring into Mary's lifeless eyes.

The bell on the door jingles, a dissonant note in the hum of the diner. In she walks—Portia Vance, a name as sultry as the lady herself. She was a stunner. The kind of dame men would fight over.

"Jake Bishop?" her voice as silky as a sunset in summer.

"What's left of him," I smile.

She slides into the booth, a coy smile playing on lips that spoke of temptation. "Portia Vance. I'm here about the job."

The smoke from my cigarette curls lazily between us. She's tall and graceful, her clear blue eyes sparkle with quick wit and intelligence. Her figure makes it hard to avoid staring. "The job's not hard, Miss Vance. Typing, filing, running errands, that sort of thing. You know how to use a datatype?"

She shoots me a look that says she can do more than type. "Comes with the territory, doesn't it?"

I grunt in amusement. "Alright, sweetheart, the job ain't glamorous, the pay's nothing to get excited about, and the hours stink, but it's yours if you want it."

She blinks in surprise. "That's it?"

"Why complicate things?" I fish a key from my pocket and place it on the table as I rise. "Start tomorrow. 442B Cooke Street."

She smiles. "I'll be there at seven sharp."

"Suit yourself, I'll be there at ten."

As I leave the joint, the rain finally stops, leaving only a steamy hot night.

I'm awake before the alarm. Nothing strange about that. I do it almost every day. Outside, the city is dark and quiet save for those other souls who, like me, have things to do at this hour. The air-brakes of a bus making it's rounds, a distant siren, a ship's horn out on the harbor. I swing my feet to the floor, grunting with the effort. Potluck, my English bulldog, casts an expectant look at me, knowing I'll fill his bowl before I even make my coffee.

A soft morning breeze wafts through the window I'd left cracked overnight, stirring the curtains and throwing odd shadows on the wall. I run a hand through my hair and stretch my aching muscles. The air, thick with summer, wraps around me as I pad to the kitchen.

Potluck follows me, his claws tapping softly on the worn-out linoleum. He does his happy dance as the kibble hits his bowl with a familiar sound. Soon he is grunting and crunching with delight.

The coffee maker comes to life, the gurgling a welcome companion in the quiet apartment. I pour myself a cup before the brew is even finished and light the day's first smoke. I boot up my datatype to check messages, its cool blue light painful to look at in the dim room. I chew a couple of aspirin absently, chasing them down with hot coffee and wait for them to go to work.

Potluck laps loudly from his water dish. His breakfast is done. I head off to the shower to wash away the last vestiges of sleep and get ready for the day. Today is the day. Today, I start the hunt for Morelli. Training, experience, intuition—they're the tools of my trade. And then there's the other thing: I'm magic. I'm what's called a *ditch wizard*, meaning no one really trained me, but like all wizards I can draw on power from *The Elsewhere* and shape it to my will. Handy stuff.

I leave Potluck in the car as I enter Bailey's. The smells of coffee and bacon welcome me as I make my way to my favorite booth. Ms. Betty, my usual waitress, brings me a hot cup of coffee and the daily crossword. "Usual?" she asks. Not to be outdone, I nod. Laconic. That's me. I dislike idle chatter before breakfast and I've always tipped her well for providing the silence.

I light a smoke and focus on my crossword, blocking out the muted conversations of the other regulars. None of my business. Just as I am pondering a five letter word for, "Deposits at the bottom of a liquid," Ms. Betty returns with a plate of bacon, a single boiled egg, and dry white toast. She refills my coffee and shuffles back to the kitchen. If they ever hand out medals for waitresses, Ms. Betty will take home the gold.

My new office is a ground floor space in what used to be a storefront of some sort. Getting blown out of a fourth story window kinda soured me on heights. The front door used to squeak something awful, but I'd taken care of that, so I enter silently. A pleasant mixture of coffee and perfume greet me. Portia, true to her word, is already in. Potluck dutifully ignores her and waddles into my private office and over to his padded bed. I walk over to where my new secretary is working.

"Settled in?" I ask. She smiles at me.

"I suppose. Kinda sparse, isn't it?", she asks.

I look around. We have electricity and light. We have a phone. Heat in the winter and cool in the summer. There were chairs, desks and filing cabinets. What more did we need? Still.

"Maybe," I allow.

"So, what's first boss?" She looks at me with an expectant sincerity.

One of Morelli's *legitimate* businesses is a dry cleaner ten blocks away. I hand her one of their business cards.

"This place, and several others, are owned by Mr. Vito Morelli. I want you to dig around, surf the electrosphere, find as many of his businesses as you can. Find out where they're located, who runs each place, and where they do their banking. Can you handle that?"

She raises an eyebrow, "That's a lot of searching, but shouldn't be too hard."

I grunt and walk into my personal office, closing the door behind me. I have my own datatype in here and I start digging into Morelli's socials. I want to get a feel for his family, his friends, and his haunts. My time in Naval Intelligence had taught me that the key to successful investigation was research. It ain't glamorous but it is necessary.

My fingers hunt and peck slowly on the keyboard. The soft hum of the datatype becomes my backdrop, Portia's distant, rapid staccato typing adds to the rhythm. A possible lead, a name—Agnes Lux. Morelli's rumored mistress. By anyone's standards, she's a knockout. Not the kind of dame a man would run off into hiding and leave behind.

The glow of the screen casts a pale light on my face as I delve into the depths of Agnes's digital life. Social media, she's fond of it. Her Sharespace page a treasure trove of information. Her profile reveals a carefully curated world—snapshots of a life intertwined with, but safely distant from Morelli.

There she is, a sultry gaze in a dimly lit restaurant, a tag revealing the location, but the entries are from before the explosion. Interesting. She went dark the same time Morelli dropped off the radar. No coincidence.

Agnes Lux, rumored mistress, a puzzle piece in Morelli's clandestine game. The screen flickers as I dig deeper, following the digital breadcrumbs.

I uncover more photos, each one telling a story. Morelli's arm around her, a stolen glance that speaks volumes. She enjoys the finer things. Upscale shopping and fine dining. A comment, joking about a 'secret hideaway.' A smirk plays on my lips.

Suddenly, Portia is looking over my shoulder. Her scent, a mesmerizing distraction.

"Find something, boss?" she inquires, refilling my coffee.

"Add the lovely Ms. Lux to your research," I instruct, pointing to my screen. "Dig into her. Likes, dislikes, friends, tastes and such. Full profile. Find out everything you can about her."

She nods, silently returning to her desk. I admire the view, and immediately chastise myself for it.

*That way layeth the minefield, Bishop.*

I light a smoke and lean back. I figure I've got enough funds to keep up the hunt for Morelli without taking on new clients for a few weeks. Morelli has a huge bounty out on him, not only from local PD but also from the Feds. Enough to cover my not earning for a while.

I open a drawer, pulling out a half-empty bottle of scotch and a treat for Potluck. I toss him the treat, which he deftly catches, and pour myself a generous slug. The booze makes a soft landing, the last tendrils of the morning headache finally letting go. I look at the clock. Noon. Damn. Those two hours had slipped by quickly.

"Ms. Vance?" I call.

She pokes her head in. "Yes, Mr. Bishop?"

"Grab some cash and pick up some lunch for us."

"Anything in particular?"

"I ain't picky."

"Back soon," she calls as she heads out.

We sit at Portia's desk, sharing a meal of something Chinese. Portia seems deep in thought, her brows furrowed as she scrolls through her datatype.

"What's got you all contemplative?" I ask between bites.

Portia looks up, a mischievous glint in her eyes. "You ever notice how women fight online? It's a special kind of battlefield. Subtle jabs and insults, passive-aggressive memes, the works. I stumbled on something interesting."

I raise an eyebrow.

"Agnes and a certain Veronica Green, they've been at each other's virtual throats. Apparently, Veronica is now dating Agnes' ex-boyfriend. Classic drama."

I set down my chopsticks. "How does this help?"

Portia smirks, her gaze fixed on the screen. "Women are vengeful. Veronica might know something, might spill the beans out of spite. It's a long shot, but sometimes people get chatty when they're angry."

I lean back in my chair, considering her words. "So, pay Veronica a visit and hope she's in the mood to dish?"

Portia nods, a sly grin playing on her lips. "Exactly. And who knows, she might know something about this *hideaway* Agnes mentioned."

"I like it." I exclaimed. "Let me know what you turn up."

"Me? You want me to talk to her? No way Bishop, I'm just the secretary, remember?"

"I have faith in you. Run it down."

"On what pretense? Why would she bother talking to a stranger?"

I focus my power and wave my hand in front of Portia. The hand-waving is not necessary for my magic to work, but I can't resist a little showmanship.

"What did you do?" Portia recoils slightly.

"It's a glamour. It will make her want to trust you. She won't know why. She'll buy any reasonable story you come up with. Now go."

Portia gives me a doubtful glance, but grabs her purse and makes her way out.

I chuckle and tidy up our lunch. Potluck enjoys the scraps.

Not one to let the grass grow under my proverbial gumshoes, I head out into the streets. I poke around a few alleys and soon find what I'm looking for. Five-Spot Freddy. A fairly harmless drunk whose brains have not yet turned to mush. The wine-soaked vagrants of Irongate have been a great tool to me in the past. Maybe my "Street Choir" can help here too.

"Hiya Five-Spot," I greet him. He raises a hand to shield his eyes from the light and gives me a gap-toothed smile.

"Mr. Bishop!" he slurs, recognition in his bloodshot eyes.

I kneel down and slide a crisp five-dollar bill into his grimy palm.

"Got a job for you, Freddy."

His eyes light up at the sight of the money.

"Sure thing, Mr. Bishop. What's the gig?"

I lean in, my voice low.

"I need you to keep an ear to the ground. I'm hunting Morelli, and I want to know if anyone's whispering about his whereabouts. Any reliable tip you bring me gets you another fiver. Spread the word—a reliable tip on his whereabouts earns a cash reward. Make sure your pals know Bishop's paying."

Five-Spot nods enthusiastically, his wiry hair bouncing with the motion.

"You got it, Mr. Bishop."

I chuckle at his enthusiasm. "That's the spirit, Freddy. Now get started. You bring me something good, and there's more where that came from."

As he pockets the bill, Five-Spot straightens up a bit.

"You can count on me, Mr. Bishop. It weren't right what they done to Mr. Frank and Miss Mary. They was always good to me, same as you. I'll see what I can shake loose."

"Thanks Freddy. How 'bout you get started *before* you spend that fiver?"

He gives me a wink and shuffles into the shadows.

It's after three when Portia returns, her cheeks flushed red and her eyes gleaming.

"So, I met Veronica. Took her for cocktails, and she spilled!" she begins, excited.

I raise an eyebrow, gesturing for her to sit.

"The glamour worked like a charm. That is one seriously bitter gal. She's pretty twisted about Agnes turning on her. Anyway, turns out Morelli has a cabin at Lake Russell, up on Cherokee Mountain. That's the *secret hideaway*! Here's the address."

Portia hands me a slip of paper, beaming with pride.

"Okay. Well done."

I give her a smile and pocket the address. Portia looks at me quizzically.

"Aren't we going to go check it out?"

"No."

"No?"

"That's right, *no. I'm* going to ride up there and nose around. I want *you* back on the banking records."

She hands me a petulant glare as I stand and grab my hat and coat.

"Make sure Potluck gets his dinner. I should be back around quitting time. Meet you back here."

The drive up to Cherokee Mountain is peaceful, the purr of the engine and the hum of the tires on asphalt my only companions. The scenery changes gradually as I climb, the city's hustle giving way to cozy suburbs and then the quiet of the mountains. The air grows crisper, and the scent of pine hangs heavy as I wind my way up the quiet back roads.

Portia's discovery about Morelli's hideaway doesn't pass the sniff test. A cabin by Lake Russell? A place concealed in the serenity of the mountains. A *well known* and *nearby* location? My gut tells me I'm on a fool's errand. Morelli, if he's there, would have to be an idiot. In this game though, you play every card you're dealt.

The road abruptly empties into a quaint little village. There's a general store, a diner, a gas station, and a post office. I punch the address into my datatype, and it dutifully shows me the shortest route. It doesn't take long.

About a quarter of a mile from the address, I park on the shoulder and get out, making my way on foot. *Cabin* is not the word I would use. It's a *huge* house with a wraparound porch nestled among the pines, azaleas, and dogwoods. A stillness hangs about the place, no smoke from the chimney, no cars in the graveled drive, no signs of habitation at all. Figures.

After a few minutes of listening and watching, I figure it's safe enough to get closer. I check the electric meter outside. Barely any movement. I find a window and peek inside. Dark. He's not here. Probably never entered his mind to come here. No, wherever the scum is hiding, it's far from the city.

The shadows are getting longer as I head back to the office. The drive back is accompanied by the same silence, while mild regret settles in. *The Hideaway* never struck me as a real lead in the first place, but stranger things have happened. I'd talk to Portia when I got back. Maybe she got something else from Veronica. Something she didn't realize was important.

Potluck greets me with an enthusiastic wag of his nub. Portia is not far behind.

"Anything?" she asks, her eyes imploring.

"Nothing. Dead end. I don't think he ever considered going there."

Portia looks crestfallen and sulks back to her desk.

"Not every at-bat gets a hit, Miss Vance. That's enough for one day. Good work. Now, go home and get some rest. We'll start fresh tomorrow."

She gives me a playful smirk and starts grabbing her things.

"Yes, Mr. Bishop."

# ACT 2: DEEPER WATERS

P otluck follows me into the apartment, his nub wagging happily. As I close the door, the sounds of the city outside are replaced by the comforting hush of the familiar space. I draw on my power and give the place a once over.

Nothing.

Clear.

No one has been here.

I set dinner on the table, takeout from a nearby wing place. Potluck plunks down nearby, his eyes watchful for the promise of a potential treat. The fragrant aroma of the food fills the room. I hang my coat and hat on the back of the door.

I reach into the bag and toss him a wing. He catches it mid-air, a display of practiced precision. I take a seat in my worn-out armchair, the day's fatigue settling in. Potluck joins me, curling up at my feet with a satisfied sigh.

Outside, one part of Irongate goes to sleep and another awakens, slowly coming alive, the flickering neon reflecting in the puddles. Absently, I chew on a chicken wing. The day's events replay in my mind—the dead-end trip to Morelli's supposed hideaway the only event of note.

I pour a splash of scotch and contemplate my next move. Morelli's pockets are deep enough to have gone anywhere in the world, but not deep enough to hide forever. Also, if he stays away for too long, it will create a power vacuum. Sooner or later someone in his organization would make a move on the old man. In the meantime, he still has to earn. He's a boss, but not *the boss*. He's gotta pay his dues. Money. It keeps coming back to the money.

I finish my meal and give Potluck the bones. As he crunches away, I pour another scotch and light another Durham. Sure, today was a bust, but it was only my first day on the hunt. Time was on my side, not Morelli's. Right now, the whispers were quiet . . . I just had to listen louder.

Portia Vance is already at her desk when I get in the next morning. I pour myself a fresh cup of brew and walk to her desk, looking over her shoulder.

"So, I think I've found all there is to find boss." She begins without preamble, leaning back in her chair. "He's got car washes, dry cleaners, pawn shops, and three restaurants. Two are dives, one is an upscale Italian place, and about four more gentleman's clubs. All of them are operating and all of them use the same bank, Summit Savings & Loan."

"Anything on his personal transactions?"

"Without hacking, I can't know more than the fact that he has an account there."

I let that one sink in and roll it around.

"Hacking, huh?"

There's something I'd not considered.

"Okay. Come into my office, we're gonna try something."

I take off my coat and hat and sit on the floor in front of my desk. I motion for Portia to join me. She sketches me a hesitant look, then kneels neatly in front of me.

"I'd like to probe your memory. I need to hear exactly what was said in your meeting with Veronica. I might pick up something that you missed and . . ."

"You want to *what*?" Portia exclaims. "I don't think so Bishop! I'm not gonna let you go rifling through my mind, prying into my every private thought! No way!"

"It doesn't work that way," I assure her. "I can't access anything you don't allow me to. If I could just mind probe people that way, I'd be the richest detective on earth! You will be aware of everything that is happening and nothing will transpire that you don't approve of."

She seems to relax a bit. At least she didn't run outta the office like Mary did the first time she saw me using my power.

After a moment of reflection, she nods her assent.

"What do I do?" she asks.

I take her hands in mine and look into her eyes.

"Just try to remember your conversation with Veronica yesterday and relax. If you want me to stop at any time, just take your hands out of mine."

I draw on my power and reach out to her, making contact easily. A thin fog clears away as I step into the memory.

*An outdoor cafe, Portia orders cocktails for them both. Skillfully, Vance engages in disarming chit chat. She asks Veronica about her falling out with Agnes Lux. Veronica spews hate-filled vitriol. Portia slides in a good one, "Why should the bitch care if you're with someone she lost?" Veronica softens a bit. She speaks warmly of her boyfriend, shares stories about their undying love. Bitterness over Agnes' hateful conduct. She was my friend! I can't believe I ever liked her! Portia offers reassurances. Veronica dishes about the hideaway. Warm goodbyes as though parting with a lifelong friend. Promises to have lunch soon.*

The memory goes dark.

I help Portia to her feet and release her hands. Her face is flush.

"That was . . ." her voice is husky with emotion. "Not what I expected."

She clears her throat, "Excuse me for a minute."

She heads off to the lavatory. One of the side effects of a mind probe is a powerful sense of intimacy. It fades quickly but can be a bit overwhelming for some.

She returns a few minutes later, looking composed. I nod in understanding. "It's not always comfortable to connect that way, but I appreciate your cooperation."

"So, did it help? Did you learn anything else?" She asks, sliding into a chair opposite my desk and absently petting Potluck.

"Nothing. Sorry to say, Veronica Greene is a dry well."

"Alright then, what's the next step?" She asks, more determined than ever.

"You mentioned hacking earlier. Got someone I want you to go see."

I hand her a card with a name and address. "Kid calls himself 'Smoke', he's a software developer who has a sideline in what we'll call, less-than-legal datatype operations. Tell him I sent you."

"What am I supposed to be asking him to do?"

"Tell him what we're trying to do, just leave Morelli's name out of it. He'll know what to do from there."

She takes the card and gives it a look.

"That's a fair way outside of Irongate. Could take a while."

"Take a couple of hundred from petty cash for Smoke's retainer. Grab yourself some lunch while you're out and I'll meet you back here later."

"What will you be doing?"

I give her a smirk of my own, "Causing trouble."

After she leaves, I make sure Potluck has plenty of water and his favorite chew toy. Where I'm going I can't take him. I don my hat and coat and make my way onto the street and turn left. It's not far and I enjoy walking. As I make my way through the concrete canyons, I again draw on my power and lay a different kind of glamour on myself. I turn up the threat. People will feel uneasy and suspicious of me. The faint of heart won't come near me. I make a right, crossing 8th Avenue and go two more blocks, left and four more blocks. *The Oasis* is on my right. I dip inside and allow myself a moment or two for my eyes to adjust to the dimness.

Only one stage running, the current girl just getting started for a small handful of gawkers. There are two rows of slot machines, a dozen tables swathed in cheap green velvet and a bar. Not more than a dozen people in the place. There's a two way mirror above the stage where management can keep an eye on things. I make my way to the bar and grab a stool.

"What'd'ya have?" A cute little number wearing a skimpy French maid's outfit with pixie short hair and too much makeup asks.

"Scotch, neat." I light a smoke and scan the place. Now that my eyes are adjusted, I can make out the muscle. Enforcers. Bouncers. Whatever. *Good.* The pixie returns with my drink and I tip her heavy. It's cheap scotch, but it's what I'm used to. I pretend interest in the show, letting the glamour do it's thing.

Magic leaves traces. A residue of various flavors. Witchcraft, Sorcery, Voodoo . . . they're all different, but they are all detectable. I reach out and take a sniff.

Nothing.

I didn't really think there would be. It ain't *that* common, but I was taking no chances. What I was doing was risky enough.

Places like the Oasis do not approve of patrons ordering only one drink and then just hanging out, taking up space and not spending. It's not as big a deal in the slow, daytime hours, but still frowned upon. Ordinarily, I might get politely asked to buy another drink or to move along. The glamour I had hung on myself all but guaranteed I'd draw interest.

After about half an hour, I feign surprise when a bouncer places a beefy hand on my shoulder, "Hey buddy, three drink minimum or ya gotta leave." Normally, a customer in this situation would either apologize and buy another drink, or would buck up and get shown the door. I needed to find a point somewhere between those two options.

"Listen, *buddy*," I replied. "I got money and time to spend, why the hassle?"

A nice middle ground I thought. What I need-ed, in case you missed it, was to get noticed poking around Morelli's operations.

"What's your name, friend?"

"Bishop, Jake Bishop." I sneer.

It was faint, but it was there. He recognizes the name. *Bingo*!

I cut him off before he can reply, "I know when I'm not wanted." I hand him my contrite routine and peel a Jackson off for the barmaid.

I leave the place and am nearly knocked down by the intensity of the sunlight. The stunt had worked flawlessly, but it would take more than one. I spend a few hours hitting Morelli's other places, making myself just enough of a nuisance to make contact with management, but not enough for things to get ugly. Most of them innocently ask me my name, the others had already gotten an electrogram about me.

So now the word is out there: *Jake Bishop is back. He's nosing around Morelli's businesses. We may have a problem.*

My feet are hurting as I leave the last dive, a particularly raunchy dump called, 'The Blue Parrot.' I step into the alley and draw on my power, opening a shadowgate that will, when I bend it to my will, open outside of my office.

Shadow-stepping can be a taxing venture. I emerge in the alley behind my office and take a minute to catch my breath. I enter the building through the service door and make my way to the office, thankful for the overworked air-conditioning. Potluck grunts and snorts an enthusiastic *hello* as I hang my hat and coat.

I don't waste any time. Morelli has already killed people I cared about when he felt threatened, and I could think of no reason why he would not try again. I needed to be ready before word went up the chain and instructions came back down.

I draw on my power again and lay my hands on the wall. I close my eyes and focus, sweat drops beading on my forehead. The spell flows through the walls, across every window and door, and even across the roof. After a moment's exertion it is done. No one could enter, by arcane means or mundane, without my knowing about it.

Perhaps I've not made it clear that sorcery is exhausting. It is. I am wiped out from the day's efforts. I make my way to my desk and collapse into my chair. What was the point of this? Somebody, somewhere is calling the shots while Morelli's away. I needed to know who. Depending on how hard I'd hit their nerves today, I'd get a "friendly" warning either later today or maybe tomorrow. Either way, both the messenger and the message would give me something to work with.

About the time I was getting ready to head out, I hear the door open.

"I'm back," Portia announces, gliding into my office.

"And?"

"And he'll send an E-gram over in the morning. Says it'll take him all night to code it."

She pauses.

"And it'll cost you a hard grand."

She looks at me nervously, as though expecting me to object.

"Fair enough. He's never burned me before and he does good work. Tomorrow morning, we'll be able to make use of all your work on tracing the money. Good job." I smile.

"Bishop," she begins with a frown. "Couldn't you have taken care of this over the phone? Were you just trying to get me out from under your feet all day?"

"No and yes." I answer. "Smoke does not like to talk business over the phone. Only in person. Yes, I needed you out of the office. I went out to stir up a bit of trouble and I didn't want to risk you getting hurt."

"Also, there were steps I needed to take to protect the office that honestly, I should have done on the first morning. They're done now so this place is as safe as any place can be." I pause. "Hand me your keys."

"I'm sorry?"

"Your keys, Portia."

She gives me a quizzical look, but reaches in her purse and hands me her key-ring. I concentrate for a moment and then hand them back.

"What did you do?"

"Anyone messes with your home or car, I'll be alerted."

"Fair enough, I suppose." She yields.

"Anything else for today?"

"No. Thanks for taking care of Smoke. See you tomorrow."

There's a quiet little corner pub in my neighborhood. I like it. Neither the Irish nor the Italians mess with the place. I'd driven home and gotten Potluck settled. Then it was time to put the second part of my plan into motion. If I was gonna be a target, I had to make myself available, so I walk the three blocks over to *The Brickyard.*

Anthony Romano is behind the bar, a tall thin gregarious man who hides a sharp mind and an even sharper memory behind a laid back affect. I slide onto my usual stool, and he pours me a generous drop of a medium-quality scotch.

"Whassup, Whassup, Bishop?" his traditional greeting.

"Same old stuff, pal," I reply.

Being the quality barkeep he is, he nods and goes on about his other tasks, leaving me in peace. I take a hard pull on the glass and enjoy the burn. I light a smoke and drag deeply. The sun is just going down, and the crowd is light. I nod to a couple of the other regulars and let the quiet happen.

A rumpled mass slides onto the stool next to me. Lt. Tom Ryan, Solomon City PD, Homicide.

His clothing, a collection of wrinkles and stains, look like they haven't seen an iron in years. The scent of old cigars wafts off of him. His watery blue eyes are rimmed in red from too little sleep or too much booze.

"Bishop," he grunts, his voice a deep stretch of gravel.

He digs in his pocket and pulls out a cheap cigar, patting his pockets for a light.

Romano steps up with a match.

"Thanks, pal."

"How's life?" I ask, sipping my drink.

Romano pulls a draft for Ryan and does his vanishing act. Ryan rumbles a low chuckle.

"Same as always Bishop, too much work, not enough pay."

He pauses to gulp half his pint in one go.

"So I got word you're back and you're gunnin' for Morelli."

"Man's gotta earn a living." I reply. "Your intel is pretty good. Only been back a couple of days."

"Yeah," a smile creases his cherub-like face, "Thing is, I'm on the case too. Difference is, if you bag him, you get a nice juicy reward. Me? I just get an 'attaboy' from the captain. Hardly seems fair." We share a laugh.

"The guy's a ghost though. Gonna be a helluva hunt." I offer. "You got anything on him?"

"Hell no." He sighs, puffing his cigar. "Just some whispers that the Russians might be looking to move on his turf, but even that's just smoke and beans. I ain't seen no indication of it."

"Yeah, I've been wondering who's holding down the fort while he's away." I offer. Ryan grunts at that.

"Good question. Tell you this too: we ain't the only hounds on the hunt," he grumbles, stabbing the air with his cigar. "Feds are sniffing around too. They want him something fierce. Local agent has a real hard on for him. RICO, OC, you know the stuff."

I toss off the rest of the glass and motion for Romano. He brings me another.

"But I'm not letting some fed take him down," Ryan declares, a hint of defiance in his weary eyes. "Morelli's my collar, not theirs."

I leave the conversation hanging there and light another cigarette, watching the thin blue smoke wander up toward the dim lights. The scotch begins to slide into that place where I relax a bit without losing my wits. I resolve to slow down so I don't miss anything.

Over the years, Ryan and I had shared info and drinks many times. I trusted him. An honest cop, and a pretty good investigator. Both rare qualities in this city.

"Make you a deal," I offer. "We share intel and I'll call you in for the bag if I find him."

His body shakes like a wool clad earthquake as he laughs.

"You were gonna call me anyway, Bishop. You know as well as I do the bastard's got half the force in his pocket. But yeah, I'll let you know if we turn anything, so long as you do the same."

"Two way street," I nod in agreement. "As long as you remember that I get the reward. I got bills to pay."

"Yeah, like you're doing this for the money." Ryan grunts.

Perceptive bastard.

We sit in silence for a long while. I distrust people who can't enjoy silence. Like, if they don't throw words out into the universe, the world will end. Ryan and I had that in common.

I walk past the frumpy used book store and the clothing store with the mannequins dressed in the latest haute couture that I've never seen anyone actually buy. I step around the pothole that's lived at the intersection for as long as I can remember, and then into my building. I gotta confess, I was disappointed that the walk home was uneventful. I kick off my shoes and get ready for bed. It's been a taxing day. I contemplate a nightcap, but decide against it. The perils of tomorrow are probably better faced without a hangover.

Tired as I am, I lie awake for a long while watching the ceiling fan cast its spider leg shadows on the ceiling and listening to the yard-trains down at the docks.

I drag the razor across my jaw, scraping away the sins of yesterday, and bang the blade on the sink. I don't bother wiping the fog off of the mirror. I know what my face looks like and there's nothing in it I want to see this morning. Scrape scrape, tap tap, scrape scrape, tap tap. The morning was doing morning things outside in the predawn.

I don't feel like breakfast this morning, so I pour myself another cup of good strong coffee and sit in my favorite chair and stare out the window. A different kind of fog lay on the view outside, a comfortable shroud muffling the moans and groans of the city.

Most people turn on the tube or the radio and get a fix of news or banter to get revved up for the day. Most people. I don't even keep a television or a radio in my home. I ain't most people. If I want news, I'll grab an old fashioned newspaper or switch on my datatype and check the electrosphere.

A subtle anticipation frets in the back of my mind. Today might be the day Morelli's goons visit me to "deliver a message." I'd give them till this evening. If they don't act, I'd just have to go make an even bigger pest of myself. I had to make sure they see a pattern in my movements. Give them an opportunity. One thing I did need to change: I'd have to get into the office earlier than normal.

I didn't want the unseen "them" to go after Portia Vance. I'd taken the initiative and hung protection spells on her car, her home, and the office itself, but they might go for her outside the office.

I have the coffee brewing and the lights on when she arrived.

"Well, good morning," She says, smiling. "This is a surprise."

"Don't get used to it, Vance." I growl playfully. "There's a lot to do today. Grab yourself some coffee and then see if Smoke sent the doohickey."

A doohickey, by the way, is a catch-all term for anything I did not understand or want to understand.

She hangs her coat and hat, pours herself a tall mug, adds cream and sugar, tosses me a wink and heads for her desk. I grab a seat in one of the chairs opposite and wait. In short order she cries out, "Jackpot!" and turns her screen to me so I can read the email:

"*Enclosed is the item you requested. There is no way of knowing how long it will take to accomplish its purpose, but it will succeed. I will send you the activation code upon receipt of the agreed upon fee.*"

"Well hell, that was fast." I quip. "Okay, wire him the money and get the thing running. Until it breaks in, that is your number one priority."

"Okay, will do, and in the meanwhile . . ."

The phone rings. *The phone*? I know this is a business and technically we're open. *How bout that*?

"Bishop Investigations, how may I help you?" she answers.

Professional ain't we? She looks at me over the handset.

"Hold on and let me check the calendar."

She puts the call on hold and looks a question at me.

I shrug, "First thing after lunch I suppose."

"Ma'am? Yes, we have an opening at 1:30 today. Yes. Yes, that's the place. Yes, the consult is free. You're welcome. See you then."

We share a chuckle. "It was bound to happen." She offers.

I'd been so caught up in Morelli that I'd forgotten that my business was still listed as "open." Just because I'm on a vendetta doesn't mean scorned wives don't need to catch cheating husbands in the act, or that business partners don't need dirt on each other. I sigh and close the door behind me as I enter my private office.

One other thing I'd neglected was the matter of Billy Scarpa, Morelli's bail-jumping nephew. The case that had started all of this. Scarpa had a nice little reward on his greasy head and I was gonna collect. I was also gonna squeeze him for every drop of info on Morelli I could get. My gut told me that Scarpa's not in hiding with Morelli. When Frank and I looked at him, we never saw any sort of close connection with Morelli. In any case, in-laws ain't blood. Scarpa had been running a couple of his uncle's paint and body shops. Turns out they were also chop shops. Little Billy had gotten himself caught, made bail and then ghosted.

My partner, Frank had found a trail of credit card receipts that placed him down in Mexico. We'd been trying to pin something more exact when the bombing had happened. The trail was cold now, but the bounty had not been cashed, so he was still out there somewhere. Little Billy was not the sharpest knife in the drawer, so there'd be clues. It was just a matter of time.

His weakness, aside from being an idiot, was a girl named Debbie Fontaine. They were inseparable. She was a thrill seeker and she wanted the world to know it. Poor dumb Billy tagged along. Fontaine posted to social media frequently. Here, they are sky diving in Jamaica, now playing roulette in Monte Carlo, now diving with hammerheads off the Mexican Coast. The last post was only two weeks ago. They were due. I set an alert on her Sharespace so I'd be notified when she posted, and decided to go grab something to eat.

I leave Portia to man the office and head to Bailey's for lunch. The special today is roast beef. I'm a sucker for good roast beef, and Bailey's does it well. Ms. Betty, who works the breakfast shift is, of course, long gone. Instead I get a bubbly young lady named Misty. Shame. I give the place a once over and see nothing out of the ordinary. I'm getting impatient with Morelli's people as I finish the meal and order a slice of pie. You'd think they'd be itching to come beat me up. Why can't criminals make my life more convenient?

The grub is as good as I had hoped. I get the leftovers in a doggy-bag and head out.

On my way back to the office, I pop in a couple of alleys and find Five-Spot. He's riper than usual and well into his own *lunch*, something in a green bottle wrapped in a paper bag.

"Mr. Bishop!" He smiles up at me dreamily.

*Great.*

"Hiya Freddie. Got anything for me?" I ask.

Yeah, Freddie is hard on the nose, but that's not the only reason I want to make this meeting quick. If I am being watched, I don't want Freddie caught up in this.

"I done just like you said, Mr. Bishop. I put the word out, but I ain't heard nothin', not a peep." he shakes his head with exaggerated remorse.

"Not a peep," he repeats.

"Okay," I reply "You go easy Freddie. Save some for dinner." I hand him the take out and pat his shoulder.

"Thanks Mr. Bishop." he calls as I make my way back into the light.

I take my time walking back, surreptitiously watching my surroundings. The afternoon is fresh and clean, the sunlight glistens on the bright chrome-clad cars. Shoppers are out on the streets, window-gazing and enjoying the day. The smell of exhaust blends with that of foods from every culture on the globe. Men in crisp suits and hats walk with ladies decked in flamboyant greens, reds and yellows. Life in the daylight.

I return to the office to find Portia behind her desk speaking with a conservatively dressed lady.

"Mr. Bishop," she begins, "This is Mrs. Lawson. She's here for a consult."

"How do you do?"

I hang my hat and coat.

"Come on into my office. Ms. Vance, coffee please."

Lawson is a striking woman, willowy with fine features, her makeup marred from recent tears. She smiles and sits down demurely as I walk around my desk and close the blinds. I light a smoke and offer her one as Portia enters with coffee for us all.

"Thank you," she says huskily, taking both.

"How can I help you Mrs. Lawson?"

Mrs. Lawson takes a moment to compose herself before she begins. Her voice trembles as she recounts the story of her missing daughter. Emily is 19, a college student with a clean record and a promising future. The desperation in Mrs. Lawson's eyes is palpable.

"Emily answered an ad for a modeling opportunity, something she had dreamed of for a long time," Mrs. Lawson explains, her hands fidgeting nervously.

"That was weeks ago, and I haven't heard from her since. We talk regularly, and she never keeps anything from me. She's never gone off like this before. I'm terrified something might have happened to her."

"With respect, Mrs. Lawson, kids that age go off on their own all the time. Do you have any reason to suspect something's wrong?"

"Oh, that's just what the police said! They said there was no hint of foul play and that Emily is an adult and can do as she likes! But I know my daughter, Mr. Bishop! She would never do this!"

She holds the cigarette to her lips with trembling hands and I light it for her.

"Alright," I sigh in resignation. I'm a sucker for the tears. "I'll look into it and see what I can find. Rate's two hundred a day, plus expenses. Do you have a photo of Emily I can keep?" She opens her purse and hands me a small photo and a blank check.

"Thank you, oh thank you, Mr. Bishop!" She smiles with weak hope.

"Look, I can't promise anything. Only that if there's something to find, I'll find it." I stand, ending the meeting. "I'll be in touch." She shakes my hand warmly and smiles at Portia.

"Thank you again!" she repeats as she exits.

"Okay Portia, you know the drill: Emily Lawson's social media, email, college records . . . all of it."

"On it boss." She quips, rising elegantly and heading back to her desk.

I look at the photo. A younger version of my client. Face a bit fuller, hair lighter. Not hard to see why modeling would appeal to her.

I close the door to my office and stretch out on the sofa. Potluck jumps up onto my lap for some petting. I absently stroke between his ears as I let my mind "professionally wander."

Over the years, I'd learned to relax and allow my mind to just go where it would when I was facing a puzzle. Concentration, I'd learned, could be over-rated.

About an hour later, Portia taps on the door and enters. I shade my eyes and squint up at her. Must have nodded off. The afternoon sun, slanting through the window, makes her features glow, almost angelic. Tall and voluptuous, blonde waves cascade around a perfect face, revealing little, hinting at more. Clear blue eyes, deep pools of mystery, and lips that could spin tales or seal secrets.

*Dammit, Bishop.*

"What is it?" I ask.

She smiles as she hands me the file, leaning in. "That's everything I could find on Emily, as far back as High School."

I take the file and move to my desk, splaying the contents out. Portia leans in over my shoulder. I can feel the warmth of her skin on my cheek.

"Nothing really jumped out at me, Jake." She begins. "She seems everything her mom says. Straight A's, Cheerleader, no serious boyfriends, school paper. She got a full scholarship to Delaine, where she's majoring in lit."

"Anything on the modeling agency?" I ask.

She leans in even further, her body pressing against mine, her left hand resting on my shoulder.

"Here," she says, her voice lowering as she turns a few pages.

"I found this on her Sharespace." *Daybrooke Modeling*, I read. She had shared a link from them, netting several replies of enthusiastic support from her followers. "It's all here."

When I turn to face her, our eyes are inches apart. Her face is flushed and I can feel her breath.

"That's good work, Ms. Vance." I breathe. "That's all for now."

Watching her leave, I face the unavoidable truth that Vance is far beyond "pretty." A dame like that! Sheesh. A body like that. Smart, witty, seductive. Dangerous! I should have waited for an old widow to answer the damned ad.

Daybrooke was a local business, it turns out. I grab my hat and coat and am out the door before any further distractions can derail me. The modeling agency is outside of Irongate, up in the more affluent Hills. The warm June air clears away the tangles as I navigate the winding avenues.

I park a couple of blocks away and make my way to the glass and granite entry. The lobby is lavishly furnished, with deep, comfortable chairs, crystal chandeliers, and thick oriental rugs. The receptionist is perched behind a mahogany desk that likely cost more than everything in my office.

"Welcome to Daybrooke," she says.

*Grace*, reads a name tag perched atop ample cleavage. Of course.

"How can I help you sir?" She smiles a vacant, uncomprehending smile. I hand her my business card and return the smile.

"Hello, Grace. Who would I talk to about aspiring talent?"

"Oh, that would be Miss Ava Harrington." She smiles, pleased, it seems, with having been asked something she could easily answer.

"If you'd like to take a seat, I'll ring and see if she is available."

"Thanks." I grab a seat and light a smoke, taking in my surroundings.

Opulence to the point of excess. Funny, I never really thought of modeling as a lucrative business. Serves me right for not being culturally astute I suppose. No denying that a nice pile of lettuce had been spent on this heap of bricks.

It wasn't long before a stunning, middle-aged woman steps over to Grace's desk and leans down to confer. A real looker. Dark curls frame a tastefully made-up face. Her navy pinstriped skirt and ivory blouse go a long way toward accenting impressive curves. Looks like Daybrooke promotes from within. She had to be a former model.

I stand as she walks over, extending her hand with a practiced smile.

"Mr. Bishop? I'm Ava Harrington. How can I help you?"

She grabs the chair next to mine and gives me a helpful smile, her emerald eyes betray a spark of curiosity. I reach into my coat pocket and produce the photo of Emily Lawson.

"Been trying to locate this young lady. Seems she had an appointment here . . . won some sort of contest," I lie.

"Her parents are worried about her. She's gone dark on them. I'm sure it's nothing, but her folks just want to be sure. You know how it is."

"My goodness!" she exclaims softly, peering more intently at the photo. "She certainly is lovely. What was the name?"

"Lawson. Emily Lawson."

"And you say she won a contest? We don't really do contests here, Mr. Bishop. Perhaps you are referring to a casting call? We do run ads from time to time looking for certain types of girls for particular contracts."

Making yourself deliberately wrong can often make people want to help you with providing correct information. It's all in the wrist, see?

"Maybe that's it. Would you have a record of it?"

"I'll be right back." She excuses herself and walks toward the bank of doors running down the far side of the place.

It doesn't take long before she returns, handing me a copy of Emily's application and a signed contract.

"Looks like she got the contract. The client's information is all there. I hope this helps."

"Did the client pay your fee?" I ask.

"Certainly," she says, handing me a copy of the canceled check.

"Thank you, Miss Harrington. You've been a help."

I head back to my car and back to my piece of the city.

At the office, I hand Portia the info I'd gotten from Daybrooke. "Run this down for me Ms.

Vance, I'm particularly interested in the client that hired Lawson, and . . ."

The door opens behind me and Detective Lieutenant Angelo Varga eases in, closing the door softly behind him. A dark, slightly built man with quick eyes and a perpetual half smile . . . always reminds me of a ferret. He takes a moment to scan the room, his eyes lingering on Portia, before settling on me.

"Hiya Bishop. Nice window dressing," he says, a lurid smile playing on his lips.

Portia rolls her eyes.

"What brings you here, Varga?" I ask.

"Courtesy call. Mind if we chat privately? Got something that might interest you."

I gesture toward the inner office, and follow him in. Once the door's closed, he gets straight to the point.

"Ever cross paths with a cat named Robert Gallo in any of your investigations?"

I shake my head, lighting a smoke. "Can't say it rings a bell. Why?"

Varga leans against my desk, his expression serious.

"I'm working a case on him. Arsonist. Likes to target cops, ex-cops, judges. I got a source tellin' me that he's the one who hit you and Frank."

"And you think we were just another target of opportunity?" I ask.

"Word is, you're still chasing Morelli for the fireworks at your office."

"Nothing secret about that," I reply, watching him carefully.

Varga sighs, a hint of frustration in his voice.

"You're not exactly being subtle about it. Rumor has it that Morelli's guys are *really* not liking you right now."

*Well well.*

He pulls a thin cigar from his coat and drags a match across his shoe to light it.

"I think you might be barking up the wrong tree, Bishop. I got reason to suspect Gallo may actually be the one behind it all on his own."

"Why would Gallo want to take me out? He got some kind of personal beef?"

He meets my gaze squarely.

"All I'm saying is, that if it's justice you're after, you might want to take a look at Gallo before you go knocking on Morelli's door."

He throws me a sly smile.

"I'd hate for you to get blown up again, y'know."

"You got something solid to show me Angelo, I'll take a look. Even if this Gallo was the torch guy, how do I know Morelli didn't put him up to it?"

"I don't know Bishop, it's your call."

He pauses and pulls hard on his cigar.

"I'm just thinking it might not be such a great idea to go gunning for Morelli when it could just be this Gallo guy doing what he does, y'know?"

He takes a few puffs on his cigar and grins.

"Maybe we can establish a little quid-pro-quo here. You keep me in the loop on what you develop, and I'll do the same."

"Gee, I'd love to help you Varga, but I got nothing. Early days. You know how it is."

He rises to leave.

"Fair enough, Bishop." He says, donning his hat.

"I'll give you a nickel's worth of free advice: *think twice about gunning for Morelli*."

"What a slime ball." Portia offers when the door closes.

"Yeah, a real charmer." I reply.

Portia stops working long enough to pull a smoke from her case.

"So what did he want, if you don't mind me asking?"

"I don't mind." I light her smoke and one of my own.

"He offered me a tip on some mutt who, he says, was the real person behind the hit on me."

"Not Morelli?" Her tone and expression echo what I'm thinking.

I chuckle.

"I don't believe it either. Got me wondering if he's in Morelli's pocket . . . low-key warning me off, or if he's dumb enough to actually believe that load he just dumped on me."

Her cigarette dangles from her full red lips as she resumes typing, and casts me a raised eyebrow.

"No," I reply to her unvoiced question. "I'm not gonna lay off Morelli."

"Good." She breathes.

"I'm gonna take off, Miss Vance. Run down that agency that hired little Miss Lawson and then close up shop. That's enough for one day."

"Okay boss," she smiles.

I decide to just grab a sandwich at The Brickyard. They do a pretty good corned beef. Romano is at the bar again, and the other regulars are all in place; like furniture that never really moves. I'm thinking over the Lawson case and toying with the idea of looking into Gallo. Not because I buy the story Varga was selling, but because if he was the one who did the actually fire-bombing, I'd want to pay him a visit too.

I take a sip of scotch that I don't remember being served, and light a smoke. Sip, puff, think. Sip, puff, think. My mind won't really focus so I decide to just shelve it all for the day. I often do my best thinking by not thinking. Sometimes, the best move is no move at all.

As I am leaving The Brickyard, they finally make their move. I confess to a moment of surprise. Though this is exactly what I've been playing toward, it still catches me off guard. Morelli's goons, a trio of cheap suits are waiting just outside the pub.

One of them, a meathead with cauliflower ears, steps forward, a menacing grin etched on his face. I keep walking and they fall in around me.

"Bishop," cauliflower-ears snarls, "You been sticking your nose into the wrong business. Yer makin' folks uncomfortable. That ain't polite. My employer sent me to ask you to back off."

I play along, a smirk dancing on my lips.

"And if I refuse?"

"Things could get nasty." He responds, his voice lowered to a near whisper.

The kidney punch from the guy behind me knocks the wind out of me and I stagger. Something hard and cold crashes above my ear and I take a knee.

I spit blood on the sidewalk and smile up at them.

"I like nasty."

The leader looks at his compatriots, hesitating for a second. A second is all I need. I move faster than their eyes can follow, grabbing the meathead by the collar, and in the blink of an eye, the world shifts. It's not a gradual fading of light and sound; it's a sudden, disorienting plunge into an abyss of freezing blackness, biting at the skin like a thousand icy needles.

Ears pop with a muffled pressure, as if the very air around us is collapsing in on itself. The silence a deafening, painful thing—a vacuum that amplifies the thudding of the heartbeat. Panic sets in as the familiar street noises vanish, replaced by the overwhelming void of nothingness.

And then, abruptly, it ends. We are standing in an abandoned warehouse, the transition so swift that the mind struggles to reconcile the freezing void with the reality of the dimly lit, musty space.

The meathead, still reeling from the shadowgate, stumbles hard, seeking stability in the unfamiliar surroundings, gasping for air. His eyes, wide with a mix of horror and disbelief, cast about, trying to grasp what has happened.

"Wh-where the hell are we?" he stammers, his voice shaky and uncertain.

I step forward and punch him hard in the gut, doubling him over.

"I'm asking the questions, asshole."

I wanted to have this over with before he had a chance to recover.

"Who told you to warn me off? I know it ain't Morelli."

He grits his teeth, gathering his resolve.

*We can't have that, now can we?* I Grab his tie and with my other hand, begin to open another shadowgate. His eyes grow wide staring into the raw chaos.

"You'll tell me what I want to know, or I swear to God, I'll throw you in and close it behind you forever!"

He spills. Bravery and machismo are all well and good in the mundane world, but they are meaningless in the face of the void. He falls to the ground and with that, I step back into the shadows, leaving the meathead alone in the empty warehouse.

It only takes a minute of searching to find the other two goons. With nothing else to go on, they had made their way to just outside of the Jewelry store below my apartment.

Their eyes widen as I step toward them, a glamour of horror emanating from me.

"Your friend is in the Bristol Warehouse on Piedmont. He'd probably be glad to see you."

I sneer.

"Now leave, while I still let you."

They take the opportunity and beat it.

I chuckle.

So now I had a name. *Dominic Santos.* It didn't ring any bells, but it's a big town and a big underworld. Wearily, I climb the dim stairs to my apartment and let myself in. Potluck greets me with enthusiasm as I make my way to the kitchen, the fatigue setting in hard. I pour a stiff one and pick up the phone.

"Portia? Bishop. Listen, I want you to make sure you lock up tonight. Morelli's boys paid me a visit just now. Got tuned up a little but, yeah, I'm fine. No, I don't think they know where you live, I just want you to make sure you're buttoned up tight. Sounds good. Okay, and call me if you need me."

I hang my hat and coat, loosening my tie and allowing the adrenaline to run off of me. My chair feels extra nice as I pour myself into it. I hold the glass in front of my eyes, allowing the neon lights outside to play in the amber liquid.

*Dominic Santos. I'll be seeing you soon pal.*

My body aches as I awaken in the predawn. Reminders of Morelli's affection, courtesy of Dominic Santos. The pounding in my skull drowns out the sounds of the city below as I swing my feet to the floor. Potluck cocks his head quizzically at my involuntary groan.

I drag myself to the kitchen, fumbling with the coffee pot, a panacea in these early hours. The wonderful aroma begins to fill the apartment as I reach for Potluck's bowl, pouring his breakfast. Leaning down costs me another wave of throbbing in my head and back.

The aspirin bottle rattles as I shake out a couple of pills, chasing them down with black coffee. The bitterness of the brew complements the bitter aftertaste of a night tangled in Morelli's web.

A hot shower offers a brief reprieve, knocking the edges of the beatings back, but dressing becomes a slow dance of agony. I can do a lot of things with my power, healing ain't one of them.

Downstairs, Potluck scrabbles onto the front seat with me as we head off to Bailey's for breakfast. The coffee, shower, and aspirin are doing a good job getting me through the worst of it. I manage to find a spot to park without too much trouble and I make my way to my usual booth. Small victories.

Wordlessly, Ms. Betty brings me a cup and the entertainment section of the paper, already folded to the crossword puzzle.

"Usual?" she asks.

I nod and take a long pull on the brew.

Good stuff.

Wonderful stuff.

The stuff of life.

Knowing she'd be in the office already, I call Portia. I want the address of the client who'd hired Emily Lawson. Figured I'd head there before going into the office.

Voicemail?

*"You've reached the office of Jake Bishop. At the tone, leave a message and we'll get back to you."*

I scowl at the phone and try again.

*"You've reached the office of . . ."* Click.

I scroll through my contacts and find Portia's mobile. No answer. A cold ball forms in my gut. I toss a Jackson on the table and run for my car.

Something had to be wrong for her to not *be* in the office. As I pull into traffic, I check . . . no messages. Dammit. Portia's place is a bungalow in the hills south of the city.

My spell . . . I check . . . still intact. No intruders. What could it be? I take the Outer Ring. It's a bit less direct, but the morning rush hour wouldn't be as bad.

I skid into the gravel driveway and run to the door. Knocking brings only silence. I move around to the back. French doors allow me to see in. She's there, on the floor, unresponsive. I grab the doorknob and focus my power. The knob and locking mechanism both shatter and I push my way in.

I kneel beside her, checking her pulse. Good.

"Portia?" I call, slapping her cheeks.

She stirs and moans.

"C'mon, Vance. Wake up!"

Her eyes flutter open, pan around, and then fix dreamily on mine.

"J-Jake?" her brows furrow in consternation.

"Yes, it's me. C'mon, let's get you off of the floor."

I lift her in my arms and lay her on the sofa. What little she's wearing leaves nothing to the imagination. I pull the afghan from the back of the sofa and drape it over her.

"What happened, Portia?"

I glance at the coffee table and there's a bottle of sleeping tablets and a bottle of brandy.

"I-I'm so sorry." She stammers. "I guess the pills were s-stronger than I thought."

I look at the date on the bottle. It's a new pre-scription. She scoots back on the sofa, sitting up. The afghan falls away as she runs her fingers through her hair.

"Never took them before. What time is it?"

"It's morning." I cup her chin and look into her china blue eyes.

The pupils are still a bit dilated. I go to her kitchen and start a pot of coffee. I find her bathroom and retrieve a robe from the back of the door.

Minutes later, I approach her with a cup and hand her the robe. She sips the former and slips on the latter.

"Thank you, Jake," she says, her voice husky.

"You had me worried. I thought maybe Morelli had . . ."

"Sweet of you, Jake. I'm sorry for the worry."

I go to her kitchen and pour myself a cup. I sit with her for a long while, making sure she's coming out of it. Outside the birds are singing and the sound of light traffic creeps into the still. In other words, it's getting awkward. She senses it too.

"I-I think I need a shower." she says, finally. "I'll meet you at the office."

"Okay, but don't rush it. Make sure you're good to drive before you head in."

The cool air blowing through the open car window is welcome as I drive back to the office. What happened to Portia could happen to anyone. Not her fault. I can't hold her responsible for anything that happened. After the scare this morning, though, I would tighten up my defensive spells around her home and car.

The sleeping pills hadn't been the only prescription on the coffee table. There was an anti-depressant and some other medicine. The label had read, "as needed for anxiety." She's been through something to need all that. Well, we all have our demons, I suppose.

Entering the office, I flip on the lights as Potluck waddles contentedly over to his bed. I make my way over to Portia's desk and begin rifling through her notes. It doesn't take long for me to find the name and address of the agency that hired Emily Lawson. Zenith Studios. Right here in Irongate. Good. I scribble a note to Portia, letting her know where I've gone.

"Hold the fort, Potluck. Back soon."

Traffic is light as I pull into a vacant spot right out front of Zenith. The place looks like any other modern edifice: all glass, chrome and granite. An attractive young lady is at the receptionist desk in the surprisingly small lobby.

"Good Morning. Welcome to Zenith. May I help you?" comes the bored greeting.

"Good morning." I return, "I'd like to see your art director."

"That would be Harry Thornton. Got an appointment?"

"No."

She shoots me the stink-eye and buzzes to the back. "Someone to see you." She says into the handset, and goes back to her datatype. Presently, a youngish man comes from the back, bedecked in a polo shirt, jeans and sandals. His thinning blond hair laid across his domed head like a threadbare rug on a marble floor.

"I'm Thornton," he says, offering his hand.

"Jake Bishop." I shake his hand and give him my business card.

"I was wondering if I could ask you about a shoot you did a few weeks back."

"Sure. Come on back to the studio."

I follow him down a long dim corridor into a big, brightly lit room filled with a menagerie of props, lights, and camera equipment. Electric cables are strewn on the floor like a nest of snakes. We thread our way through all of this to a sofa and chairs in the corner.

He twists the top off of a bottle of water and takes a swig.

"How can I help?" he asks.

I hand him copies of the contract provided by Daybrooke and the photo of Emily.

"This is Emily Lawson. The young lady has gone missing. Was hoping you might be able to tell me about the shoot."

"What would you like to know?"

"Anything you can give me would help."

He blinks a couple of times.

"Well, it was a clothing catalog shoot. Nothing out of the ordinary. New fall fashion stuff for Suitecliff's. Took most of the day as I recall. The young lady did a great job for a rookie. A real natural."

"Was anyone with her?"

"No. She came on her own."

"She say or do anything that stood out to you?"

"No. Just chit chat about college and modeling. Normal stuff."

"Forgive my ignorance, but is it just you doing the shoot?"

"Heck no. There's a whole crew in here when we're shooting. Plus, when the model's a female, I always have Janet, or Rhonda—our receptionist—in the room."

"Crew?" I ask.

"Janet does makeup, Barton does the lighting, and Benny does the props. I take the pictures and direct the shoot."

"Anyone else?"

"Not usually. Our owner, Mr. Giovanni popped in, but he does that a lot."

"I see. Did the shoot come out alright?" I ask, lighting a cigarette.

"Oh yeah. Suitecliff's was happy. I do good work Mr. Bishop."

"If you don't mind my asking, how much does the model get for a catalog shoot? You said it took most of a day?"

"Pretty standard rates. About five-hundred for the whole thing."

Thornton seemed as eager to give information as I was to get it. The problem was there wasn't a lot of water in what was obviously a shallow well.

"Okay, thank you Mr. Thornton." I rise and shake his hand.

"If you think of anything later, give me a call."

I don't wait to be escorted out. I make my way through the obstacles, down the dim hallway, through the undersized lobby and back into the real world. I never really cared for the artsy type anyway.

*Giovanni*. Could be a coincidence.

Probably not.

I call the office, hoping Portia has pulled herself together and gotten in. I'm not disappointed.

"Bishop Investigations," she answers. Good.

"Ms. Vance, Zenith is owned by someone named 'Giovanni'. I need everything you can dig up on him as quick as you can.

"I'm on it. Are you coming in?"

"Not yet. Got some things to run down first."

I head downtown. I don't enjoy visiting the Police Department, the place reeks of misery and too much bureaucracy, but I need information.

The place is alive with activity, the lobby choked with victims looking for help and perps crying about their rights. The dozens of conversations and ringing phones in the bullpen is a painful cacophony. A thick layer of cigarette smoke hovers like fog over London. I nod to a couple of officers who know me, making my way to the glass-walled offices in the 'Major Crimes' department.

"Bishop!" Ryan greets me through puffy red-rimmed eyes, his stubble-covered jowls spread into a smile. "Grab a seat."

"Thanks pal."

I sit down and pull a smoke from my coat pocket. Ryan reaches into a drawer and pours some bourbon into a spare mug and passes it to me.

"So, what brings you to my little slice of hell?" He asks.

"Ran across a name I'm not familiar with. Wanted to run it by you."

"The Morelli case?" He asks, hopefully.

"No. Missing person case."

"Why come to me? That's something for the General Investigations Unit."

"Just a shot in the dark. The name that popped up? It's Giovanni. I know you handle OC."

I nearly choke on the cheap bourbon.

"I see." He says. "Pretty sure that asshole has come up once or twice."

He bangs away with two fingers on his datatype. His already beady eyes narrow even more as he reads.

"Yeah. Here he is. Owns a photo studio, a moving company, and deals in real estate."

"That's the guy."

"Hmm. Rumored to be connected to . . . of course . . . Morelli."

"Of course." I agree.

"We were looking at him for . . . looks like . . . distribution. Moving dreamdust. Nothing developed. Creep got a mouthpiece and got a cease and desist from the right honorable Judge Wilson. Case moved to inactive."

"Shit. Okay. Thanks."

"Problem?"

"The missing person is a college kid, Emily Lawson. Last seen at Zenith Studios. Giovanni was there when she came in for a photoshoot."

I frown hard. I'm good at frowning.

"I don't like this."

"I hear you pal." He taps a couple of keys and his printer squeaks to life, spitting out a small stack of paper.

"So what's your move?"

"I suppose I got no choice. I gotta pay the mutt a visit."

"I wish I could help ya on this one Bishop, but without something to take to a judge, I'd only slow you down."

He hands me the pages from the printer.

"Hope this helps."

I toss off the last of the bourbon and take the pages.

"Thanks Ryan, I owe you."

Portia looks as put together as ever when I enter the office. No trace of her difficulties from this morning.

"Tell me something good." I call as I head for my office, Potluck waddling beside me.

The air conditioning feels good as I hang hat and coat on the back of my door.

Portia enters with a file and a cup of coffee for me.

"That's everything I could find." She smiles.

"Jake. About this morning . . ."

"Forget it, doll. Accidents happen. Leave it alone."

She nods and slides into a chair opposite my desk.

"What's our interest in this Giovanni guy?" She asks, lighting a smoke.

I relate everything I'd gotten from Zenith and from Ryan.

"That's no coincidence," she offers.

"You're right."

I flip through the papers Ryan gave me, comparing with the stuff Portia downloaded.

"This address? See if you can get street views and aerial shots. I want to take a look at the place before I resort to direct confrontation. If he's got Emily, maybe I can leverage that for info on Morelli in addition to getting her out."

"Okay but what if . . ."

"What if she's not there? Or, what if she's there of her own free will?"

Portia nods.

"I'll cross that bridge when I get to it."

"Okay, let me see if I can find those shots you want."

She heads back to her desk. I lean back, reading the files. Finally something to act on.

Probably.

Hopefully.

Portia finds me an address up in the Palisades close to Giovanni's place. The homes up here likely cost more than the whole street I live on. Thirty minutes later, I pull into the curved drive of a starter-castle with a "For Sale" sign by the curb. I grab my binoculars and head for the back of the place. The trick is to walk like you belong. No sneaking.

My perch is considerably higher than Giovanni's place. I take out the binoculars, and pan around. Tennis court, manicured grounds, and a pool. There! By the pool. I focus the lenses. Yes, it's her. Emily Lawson, lounging by the pool sipping something exotic, chatting away on her phone. She's notably more tanned and toned, but it's her. She's no prisoner.

On the drive back, the bile rises in my gut. The bitter taste of defeat. I mean, I found the girl, and that's what I was hired to do . . . so why the black mood that was riding along with me though the winding hills?

Maybe it's the realization that my hunch about Giovanni was wrong. Maybe it's the frustration of not uncovering the sinister plot I had imagined, and the opportunities it would have offered. Or perhaps it's the stark contrast between Emily's apparent freedom and her mother's tearful concern. Either way, it doesn't feel like success.

Still, I owed it to my client to see it all the way through. I'd get Portia to do that part.

I pour myself a stiff one and prop my feet up on the desk as Portia dials the number.

"Yes, is Emily there please? Tell her it's Kate from Daybrooke Modeling Agency. Yes, I'll hold."

Portia lights a cigarette and locks eyes with me.

"Emily? Hi. You don't know me, but I'm a friend. I just wanted to know if everything is okay with you? You're mother has been worried sick and . . . Yes."

Portia frowns for a long pause as Emily speaks.

"Yes. I see. I won't bother you again. Yes, I'll tell her." Portia hangs up the phone and exhales deeply.

"What is it?"

"She's not interested in talking to her mother or anyone else. Seems her mother, our client, remarried after Emily's father passed. The new step father couldn't keep his hands and eyes off of Emily. Emily told her mother . . ."

"And Mother didn't believe her. So our Miss Emily took the first opportunity to bail." I finish the story.

"Completely unaware that she's shacked up with a different kind of monster." I shake my head.

"A lousy situation, Miss Vance."

"Lousy," She affirms.

I work through lunch, poking around the electrosphere for Debbie Fontaine. I had alerts set if she posted to Sharespace, but so far I'd netted a big fat nothing. She and Scarpa were due to pop up somewhere interesting. Giovanni had wriggled off the hook, or more precisely, never got on it in the first place. Scarpa would not be so lucky. All I had to do was put hands on him. The warrants were already in place.

It would be nice if the two of them popped up somewhere close by. Close by, in this context, meant anywhere in this hemisphere. At least that was the greatest distance I had ever shadow-stepped. And I have to know where I am going. I was grasping at straws. There was simply nothing to be found. The frustrations just kept piling on.

The buzzing on the intercom startles me.

"Mr. Bishop? Someone here to see you."

I step into the reception area and am greeted with the smell first. It's Five-spot.

"Hiya, Freddie. Got something for me?"

"Yes, Mr. Bishop I sure do." He smiles.

"You gonna make me wait?"

"Well, it's like this. A buddy of mine was doing some day labor down at the docks, and get this, a suit comes up to him and says, 'Can you get word to Jake Bishop?' So my pal, he says, 'Yeah' and the suit tells him to get word to you that Santos wants to meet with you."

"Okay. Did the suit say when or where?"

"No Mr. Bishop, that's all of it." Five-spot clutches his hat in both hands, his eyes imploring.

"Alright, Freddie," I pull out my wallet.

"Here's ten for you and five for your pal. Make sure he gets his."

"I will! I hope it helps you Mr. Bishop. I really do." He's just as sincere as hell.

I pat him on the back and usher him out the door.

"Thanks Freddie, you take it easy now."

As soon as the door closes, Portia is spraying disinfectant with one hand over her nose and mouth.

"Kinda refreshing ain't he?" I laugh.

"Christ, Bishop. We may have to burn the place to the ground to get that smell outta here."

"No thanks. One torched office is enough for one lifetime."

"Oh crap! I'm sorry Jake, that was thoughtless of me." She seems genuinely mortified.

"Forget about it." I offer. "Is the gizmo still trying to break into Morelli's accounts?"

"Yes, it's still running. I've got it set to alert me when it breaks in."

"Okay."

I sit down in one of the leather chairs opposite her desk and scowl at the linoleum. Portia gracefully slides behind her desk, her eyes asking me for instructions.

"I want you to call Mrs. Lawson. Tell her we found Emily and that she is alive and well, but does not wish to be contacted. If she pushes, you can tell her about your conversation with Emily."

Portia frowns, but nods. No one enjoys being the bearer of bad news.

"After that, type it all up and file it in the closed cases. Send her an invoice and deposit the check."

I rise with a groan and grab my hat and coat.

"When you're done, you can knock off for the day."

"Okay Jake." she smiles warmly.

Santos wanted to meet. Okay, I'm game. If he wanted to cause me harm, he would have just sent some more muscle. Ditto if he just wanted to send another "message." No, he wants to put eyes on me . . . to sound me out and get a feel for what I'm after. He didn't specify a location, which means he expects me to find him in a place he's known to frequent.

I'd memorized the legitimate businesses Morelli owns and there's only one place that seemed appropriate. He'd be at Vinzo's for dinner.

Fine. I like steak.

I head for home so I can get cleaned up and drop Potluck off.

The place oozes opulence, a stark contrast to the greasy spoons I frequent. The maître d' gives me a side-eye as if I might stain the expensive linen just by being here. Hell, maybe I will. I was in a gilded snake pit, but it was snake pit nonetheless.

"Here to see Santos," I tell him and breeze past him before he can object.

In the dim light, I spot him. He's the picture of calm, savoring a glass of something red. He's a tall, polished patrician with thick black hair, narrow dark eyes, and a pencil thin mustache, red silk tie, and grey shark skin suit. Pure panache.

"Hello, Santos," I open, slipping into the seat across from him. "Nice place."

Santos raises an eyebrow, a fractional twitch of a smile breaks his stoic expression.

"Hello, Mr. Bishop. I'm glad you could come on such short notice." he acknowledges, raising his glass.

"Wine?" He motions to a waiter.

"Yes, please."

The gloved waiter pours for me.

"A nice little Merlot we stock. I think you'll appreciate it."

I order a rib-eye, and the waiter vanishes. The tension is there, but we both know the rules of this game. Things will be *civilized* unless I commit a gross breach of etiquette.

"Business treating you well, Mr. Bishop?" Santos drawls, twirling the stem of his wine glass casually.

"As well as can be expected. You know how it is, always chasing the next pay check." I match his tone, casual as a Sunday afternoon stroll.

"How're things in your world?"

Santos leans back, a cat contemplating a mouse. "Steady, Mr. Bishop. Steady. No complaints."

He'd asked for the meeting, so the agenda was his to set.

"Steady is good," I agree, keeping the conversation floating on the surface while we both dive for the depths.

"Speaking of, I hear your boss is on extended holiday. I hope he's well."

Santos's gaze narrows, and he chuckles. "A change of scenery can do wonders for the soul."

"True, true," I reply, sipping the Merlot.

Santos wasn't lying about the wine. It's very good.

"I imagine the extra work has got you busy, though."

The steak arrives, a sizzling distraction, and we both dig in, allowing the suspense to marinate.

"I enjoy it, Mr. Bishop, and hard work never hurt anyone."

I glance at him, chewing slowly, savoring the layers of meaning in his words. "Maybe. But you know what they say, 'all work and no play' . . ."

He smiles a reptilian smile.

"I asked you here, Mr. Bishop, to let you know that I personally take no offense with your current line of inquiry. We all do what we feel we must and, after all, change is inevitable."

In case you missed it, Santos was letting me know that he only sent the goons after me because Morelli had ordered it.

"I appreciate that, Mr. Santos." I lie.

"And for my part, I bear no hard feelings over the delivery of your last message. I understand how these things work."

He nods.

So, I was reading this correctly.

"And where did you say he was taking his holiday?"

Clumsy. I regret it as soon as I ask it.

"I didn't." Santos shakes his head, smiling. "But I can appreciate your curiosity."

And just like that, Santos has told me he won't interfere with my going after his boss. He knows the score. He knows I'm no threat to his organization, and that removing his boss would only benefit his standing, but he won't roll on Morelli.

I raise my glass, "To understanding."

He smiles and raises his glass in agreement.

"The dinner is on me. Until next time, Mr. Bishop," Santos says, ending the meeting.

"Until next time," I echo.

The blinds are casting long, sharply angled shadows across the walls when I get home. I'd be lying if I said I wasn't relieved that Santos wasn't gunning for me. Sure, I can handle most hostilities, but a rooftop sniper or another firebombing would be something else entirely.

I pour myself a tall scotch, light a smoke, and crack open the window. I enjoy the sounds of the city riding in on a cool breeze that smells of auto exhaust and the sea. As I collapse into my chair, my thoughts go back to the days following the explosion that nearly ended my life. Tom Ryan was assigned to the case. Came to see me in the Intensive Care Unit and told me they'd caught the mutt that had done the actual bombing. Irwin McCall, he'd informed me, was a known arsonist. He'd confessed, rolled on Morelli, and then promptly stabbed himself in the kidneys multiple times while in holding. McCall. Not Gallo, like Varga said.

There was nothing forensic to tie the event to Morelli and of course he denied any involvement. Had an airtight alibi too. The theory Ryan was working with, and I couldn't fault his reasoning, was that Morelli hadn't quite bargained for the size of the bang he got for his money. It claimed the lives of my partner, Frank Donovan, and Mary, our secretary—the widow of a cop who bit it in the line of duty, she was the sweetheart of the Police department. Frank was a retired vice lieutenant. The whole affair cranked up the heat—forgive the crude pun—so Morelli decided to vanish until his expensive lawyers and even more expensive politicians could sweep it under the rug.

"Over my dead body," I mutter to the silence.

Investigation is a strange profession. Most cases are dirt simple. Get some incriminating photos. Trace a bail jumper. Dig up dirt on a business rival. Other cases, like this one, are like baseball; you fail more often than you succeed, even when you're winning.

Agnes Lux, Dominic Santos, Emily Lawson, Billy Scarpa . . . the strikeouts were piling on. Was I winning? What the hell kind of name was *Lux* anyway? Too tired to think, I make my way to the bed and give up the day. I fall asleep thinking about baseball and batting averages.

The next few days are a blur of activity without result. I am a patient man. Hell, waiting is a big part of the job, but after a while, it gets tiresome. Finally, late on a Friday, I get an alert from Fontaine's Sharespace. She and Little Billy Scarpa are going conch diving in Key West! Itinerary says they are flying down from New York with a layover in Atlanta. You can't die and go to Heaven without a layover in Atlanta. Perfect. I call the office and tell Vance that I won't be in until late. I grab my hat and coat and open a shadowgate.

Airports are wonderful places for covert operations. They are busy, noisy, crowded, and everyone is so focused on getting from point A to point B that they don't really watch their surroundings. I'm watching the herds of people flowing into the gate for Key West. As I sit in the dimly lit corner of the airport lounge, the rhythmic hum of chatter and the occasional clinking of glasses go largely unnoticed. I glance at my watch for what feels like the hundredth time, its hands creeping closer to the appointed hour. Any time now.

My eyes scan the crowd, searching for a familiar face in the sea of strangers. And then, they are there. Little Billy, with his slicked-back hair and a nervous energy that seems to ooze from every pore, walks arm in arm with Debbie Fontaine. She's a vision in pink, her lips painted scarlet and her curves wrapped in a light sundress.

I watch as they approach the boarding gate, their footsteps echoing against the polished floors. Little Billy casts furtive glances over his shoulder, trying to hide the paranoia etched into every line of his face.

Debbie clings to his arm, her eyes darting around the terminal taking it all in, oblivious to her lover's fear. I rise from my seat, and fall in behind them.

As I draw nearer, I can feel the tension crackling in the air like electricity. Scarpa looks back over his shoulder, his eyes lock with mine, and for a moment, time stands still. There's a flicker of recognition in his eyes, followed by a flash of fear. He knows he's trapped. I smile in spite of myself.

With a practiced calm, I grab him by the collar.

"Scarpa," I say, keeping my voice low. "I believe we have some unfinished business."

Debbie lets out a gasp of surprise, her nails digging into Billy's arm as she tries to pull him free from my grasp. I gesture with my free hand, opening a shadowgate back to my office and shove Little Billy through. I glare at Fontaine as she recoils in shock.

"Run along, Ms. Fontaine. There's nothing here for you anymore."

I step through the gate and close it behind me.

Back in the safety of my office, Scarpa is sitting on the floor trying to recover from the shadowgate. His eyes are blinking rapidly as he takes in his surroundings. Wordlessly, I grab his elbow and guide him into my private office and deposit him in a chair. I lock the door behind me and sit behind my desk. I pour myself a glass of celebratory scotch and light a smoke. Being on the run for so long has taken a toll on Scarpa. His eyes are bloodshot, with dark rings underneath, he's lost weight, and didn't have enough to spare to start with.

"I know you." He says. "You're that detective that got blown up."

"Yeah, that's me. Your uncle Vito tried to kill me. He shoulda made sure, don't you think?" I smile. "Shame about that."

Scarpa's eyes scan the room, looking for an out. He licks his pale thin lips.

"Look, I had nothing to do with that. I don't know anything about it! Just let me go. I can pay you!!"

"I know you had nothing to do with it, Billy. I'm turning you in for the bounty, that's all."

I take a pull off the scotch and dangle a carrot.

"Hell, with your connections you'll probably be bonded right back out. You and Fontaine will be in Key West before you know it."

I stub out my smoke and lock eyes with him.

"Of course, that's assuming you get to the lockup in one piece." I give him my best glare.

"You know what I am. You've seen what I can do."

His eyes go wide as raw panic sets in.

"W-What are you gonna do? What do you want?"

I make him wait for it. He is shaking now, fear wrapped around him like a heavy coat.

"Hell Billy, all I want is your Uncle. Give me his location and you can walk right out of here."

"B-but, I don't know where he is! He ain't told me nothing!! I got no idea!"

"Oh come on, Billy. Surely you know him well enough to make an educated guess."

"It ain't like that with us man! We ain't close. He don't tell me nothing!"

I begin tracing small circles in the air between us, causing tiny sparks to sizzle and pop.

"Having a hard time believing you Billy. You two were close enough for him to firebomb me to keep you safe. You're gonna tell me he never took you to one of his hideaways?"

Outside my door, I hear Portia open the outer door and walk to her desk, heels clipping and keys rattling.

"No man, you got it all wrong," He stammers. "He only did all that cause my mom asked him to. I swear it man, I don't know where he is. I got no idea!!!"

He is almost squealing now, his eyes locked on the little light show I'm performing.

The intercom buzzes.

"Jake, is that you in there?"

I stop the light show and push the button, "Yeah, it's me. Do me a favor and call Lt. Ryan down at the precinct and tell him I've got Billy Scarpa in my office."

"Will do." She replies.

"Okay Billy, I believe you." I drop the light show in bitter disappointment.

"Go and handle your business like a man and maybe you and Fontaine can actually have a life together when you get it all sorted out."

I lean down and look into his eyes, "But if you ever cross my path again, I'll burn you to ashes."

I draw on my power and shackle Scarpa to the chair, and walk out to Portia's desk. I can't stand looking at the little punk anymore.

As Lt. Ryan and the two officers lead Scarpa out in cuffs, I turn to Portia. "Vance, close up shop, go home and get dolled up, we're gonna celebrate this evening."

Her eyes widen in surprise, a flicker of astonishment quickly replaced with a mischievous grin.

"Sure, Boss!" she replies.

With a quick nod, she reaches for her bag. We douse the lights and lock the place up.

"I'll pick you up at your place, six o'clock," I tell her.

There's a fantastic seafood place called Salter's on the edge of the pier district. Here's a little free advice that's always served me well: when you find a place that does everything right, and where the seats are hard to come by, and you'd like to enjoy the same experience again, tip big. Over the years I'd dropped in often enough, and tipped large enough, to get remembered by name. The Hostess greets me and shows us to a little two-seater in the corner, away from most of the noise. Our waiter wordlessly hands us menus. I order a scotch, neat, for myself. Portia opts for a gin and tonic.

At the really nice places, a sommelier will arrive and present the wine choices for the evening. I take his recommendation for a chilled Riesling. As we wait for our drinks, I wave the waiter over. I settle on the lobster bisque to start, followed by the grilled halibut with lemon butter sauce for the main. Portia's eyes light up as she orders the seared scallops with risotto.

Salter's exudes lavishness in every detail. Soft lighting accentuates mahogany furniture and gleaming silverware. Plush velvet curtains frame the towering windows, while crystal chandeliers cast shimmering light. The tables boast crisp white linens and delicate stemware while a band croons out soft jazz.

"Pretty posh, Boss." Portia opines, showing me her dimples.

"Don't get used to it, Vance. We're gonna be eating a lot of takeout until we bag Morelli."

I take a long pull on my scotch, enjoying the warmth it spreads though my body and lighting a smoke. I light one for Portia which she takes with a thanks.

"But I always celebrate closing a big one. This whole mess started because of Scarpa. Nabbing that mutt is cause for celebration."

"Here's to more success then." She raises her glass.

We share a dance on parquet floor. Her scent is intoxicating, her body, soft and lithe in my hands. Her eyes are locked onto mine, her lips, so close to mine are inviting. She leans in, ever so slightly. I'm damn close to giving in but stop myself. I can't let myself get that close to her!

Nothing happens . . . barely.

By the time we're having coffee and dessert, I'm in a pretty good place. Portia is all smiles and laughter. A pretty nice outing. We collect our things from the coat check and step out into the night. The temperature has dropped a bit and a light rain is pattering down on the asphalt.

Suddenly, a dark coupe barks to a stop right in front of us. Portia screams a warning and, before I can react, something hard happens to the back of my head. I see stars, stagger forward, and then all goes black.

I regain consciousness slowly, as a dimly lit room swims into focus around me. Racks of plastic-sheathed clothing hang from carousels, a chemical odor hangs heavy in the air, mingling with the musty scent of old fabric. I'm in the back of a dry cleaner's shop.

My head throbs as I become aware of my bindings, the rough rope digging into my wrists and arms. Weakly, I struggle against them, my movements feeble against the tight knots.

I attempt to summon my magic, but to no avail. It's like hitting a brick wall, a barrier that prevents me from tapping into the energy that powers my abilities. Confusion clouds my mind as I realize something—or rather, someone—is blocking me.

Perched atop a stool in the corner, I spot an older black man with white hair and a deeply weathered face. He's dressed in a white T-shirt and jeans, with a pendant hanging around his neck. He's a shaman, a practitioner of voodoo, and he's hung some kind of warding to block me from reaching into *The elsewhere*. Shaman. Of course. I hate those guys. Someone's done their homework on me.

I strain against the ropes, my heart pounding in my chest. And then, they materialize from the shadows—two figures, their silhouettes menacing in the dim light.

One of them, a towering brute with knuckles wrapped in tape, fixes me with a cold, unyielding gaze. His eyes gleam as he strips off his tie and shirt, muscles rippling in the faint glow, a cruel smile twisting his lips.

"Hiya, Bishop," he rumbles, "Hope you had a nice dinner."

Benny "The Brick" Rossi. I'd seen him around Irongate. Freelance enforcer for the outfit.

The other, a lean and wiry little guy with a jagged scar running down his cheek, gives a short, sharp laugh.

"Probably the last solid food you're gonna have for a while."

I don't know this one, but he's holding a snub nosed .38 by his side.

I swallow hard, the taste of dread bitter on my tongue. I know what comes next. This isn't any interrogation—they're here to deliver a message. My only comfort is knowing that if they wanted me dead, they'd have just put one in the back of my head and avoided all this theater.

I meet their menacing gazes head-on, feigning a toughness I don't really feel.

"Hiya Brick. Dinner was great, but the enter-tainment is lousy. You boys should work on that."

I nod toward the shaman.

"The chicken-foot is a nice touch. Where'd you find him?"

Brick smiles knowingly. "You like that? We asked around down in Little Carib, Teddy here came highly recommended."

The little one leans down to look me in the eye.

"He don't look so tough to me, Brick. I thought he was supposed to be dangerous."

"Not as dangerous as your breath, punk. You been eating roadkill or something?"

Little Guy's head jerks back at my quip and he throws a quick shot to my jaw.

"You got bad manners, tough guy." He spits on the concrete floor. "That's another thing we're gonna have to beat outta you."

"You better let Brick do the beating, little man, you hit like a dame."

Brick chuckles.

I focus and try to force my way through the warding. Teddy flinches on his stool.

"Aye man, he's a strong one, this guy." He says, grasping the amulet.

Brick steps up, pushes Little Guy aside and gives me a proper right cross. Stars dance before my eyes and there's a deafening ringing in my ears. He follows with a left and I can feel myself fading.

Little Guy leans in and says, "Y'know, the boss doesn't even like little Billy. Can't stand him, really. The kid's a turd, but he's the boss' nephew. Family, see?"

He raises up and lights a thin cigar.

"Seems to me you got some kinda learning problem, Bishop. You start diggin' into Scarpa and your whole office gets creamed and what do you do? As soon as you're walking again, you go right back after him. Not real smart."

"Like you said, I learn real slow." I breathe out.

So this came down from Morelli, not Santos. Interesting. I file that away.

"Enough chit chat," says Brick. "Figure if we put you back in the hospital for a few weeks, that'll help you figure things out."

He hands me a thorough beating. I've been roughed up before, but this one was a real masterpiece. Blood is pouring over my left eye as Brick grabs a bat and steps forward.

*Oh shit.*

Just as he's drawing back to deliver, a bullhorn calls out, "This is the SCPD, you're surrounded. Drop your weapons and get on the floor!"

Little Guy calls out, "Scram boys!" and he puts action to words as he, Brick and Teddy run. I can't see where they go. Too dark, and my left eye is swelling shut. Several pairs of shoes scuffle into my periphery.

"Jeez." Someone hisses looking at my busted face. "Get the medics in here."

"Hang in there, Bishop," says Ryan. "We're gonna get you fixed right up."

*That's good to hear,* I think. *A good plan.*

I rise slowly from a narcotic induced haze, greeted by the smell of disinfectant and the distant beeping of monitors. The room is dark, the only light falling in bands of light and shadow from the window. I'm in a hospital. An all too familiar setting. My mouth is dry, parched like the cracked earth in a long, summer drought. I try to turn my head to find the water bottle or the call button, but I can't move. Got a C-collar wrapped around my neck.

"What do you need Jake?"

It's Portia, sitting quietly by my side for God knows how long.

"Water," I mumble.

I hear the sound of her pouring a cup. "Here." A straw presses against my lips and I sip. Amazing how such a simple thing can bring so much relief.

"How long?" I whisper.

"Not long, Jake. It's almost sunrise."

So I've been out for hours, not days. That's a good thing, I suppose. Better than the last time I woke up in a similar room.

"When they grabbed you, I got a cab and followed. I called Ryan. You know the rest," she says. "I'm sorry it took so long."

I struggle to sit up in the bed. My body complains loudly about battered bones and muscle, but I manage. Portia clicks on a lamp by the bedside.

"You've looked better." she smiles wanly. "How do you feel?"

"Terrible. What do the docs say?"

"Nothing broken. Couple of stitches above one eye. They wanted to admit you for observation. Concerned about a possible concussion."

Right on cue, the door opens admitting more light and a doctor. He shines a light in my eyes, causing me to wince, and listens to my heart. He checks the chart and decrees, "I think we can cut you loose after breakfast. You're gonna need to take it easy for a few days. I'll write you something for pain."

"No drugs." I snap. "I'll be fine without 'em."

"Suit yourself." Great bedside manner that guy.

I spend the next couple of days chasing aspirin with coffee in the mornings and scotch in the evenings. Portia's in and out a few times a day, hustling takeout and smokes. If she's bucking for a raise, she's doing it right. I keep the office pretty much shut down. Let Morelli's boys think I'm worse than I actually am. Witches and Shaman, I'm told, can use their art to heal. Wizards, not so much. At least not that I've ever heard about. So I gotta rely on time and a pretty good constitution.

The question that keeps tumbling around my mind is who Morelli worked through to arrange my beating. Santos is in charge while Morelli is on the lamb, and not the type to look kindly on someone else over-stepping their bounds. No chance Morelli would directly contact someone else in his own outfit. So, either Santos ordered it on Morelli's instructions, in which case, he's broken our unspoken truce, or Morelli has someone else on the hook. Neither choice is particularly attractive.

I can only stay cooped up for so long so, a week after my tune-up, I'm headed into my office. One more day of staring at the same four walls and I'd be ready to start eating paint chips. I'd called Vance the night before and told her we were back on the clock. True to her nature, she's in the office when I arrive, even though I'd made the effort to be earlier than usual.

Potluck snorts loudly, waddling over to Portia, receiving her attention with bulldog enthusiasm. The coffee smells inviting and I walk into the little room where we brew it and where we keep the files. I pour a generous mug and limp over to a chair opposite Portia's desk.

I lay out my current puzzle for Portia, and she asks the obvious, "How do we know Morelli didn't order Santos to do the deed?"

I don't quite know how to answer her. The odd thing is, in spite of their criminal activities, most of the Mob families are pretty strict about their code of honor. A man's word is supposed to be iron clad. I just couldn't see Santos pulling something like this.

"Set that aside for the time being. Assume it wasn't through Santos. Who else would Morelli reach out to?"

Portia lights herself a smoke, her brows furrowed.

"Could be anyone if you think about it. Why not just call one of his boys up and tell him to do it directly?"

"Doesn't work that way. If he stepped over Santos, Santos would be justified in making a move on Morelli himself. With Morelli out of town, and Santos holding all the strings locally, it would be simple for Santos to take over. Mob bosses don't fear the local cops or even the feds, but they do fear their own lieutenants."

"Pretty messed up way to run things." Portia quips, sipping her coffee and lighting a smoke of her own.

"You're right, but that's the way it is."

A thought occurs to me and I call Lt. Ryan. I ask him to send me everything he's got on Benny "The Brick" Rossi.

"I figured you'd want that." He laughs, "It's already in your D-mail."

"Serves me right for not being technologically inclined." I laugh.

I point to the datatype on Portia's desk. She gets the cue and opens the connection.

"That's two I owe you pal. Thanks."

"Just two?" he scoffs. "Don't mention it. Hope it helps." He ends the call.

I step around Portia's desk and point "That mugshot? Can you send it to my phone?"

She nods and does it in less time than it took for me to ask the question. I check my phone to make sure I'd gotten it.

"Thanks, Doll. I'm out for a few. Hold down the fort."

I head out and hit a few contacts, looking for info about who Rossi has been working for. Last I'd heard, he was freelance muscle for whichever mid-level boss needed him. That jibes with my theory that Santos didn't order my abduction, but it also makes it hard to know who Morelli might be working through.

I drop into a handful of beer joints and hangouts to spread a little dough around. It's a ham-fisted way of doing things, but it's all I've got at the moment. Lot's of informants, street rats, and thugs know Rossi, but no one knows who he's working for at the moment. By the time I'm done, the word is out that I'm looking for the information. All I can do now is wait.

I hate waiting.

By the time I make it back to my side of Irongate, my feet are killing me and I'm in a foul mood. I'm walking the last block back to my office when I set eyes on one of the local toughs walking toward me from the opposite direction. I recognize the guy as a bouncer at one of Morelli's clubs, Marco something-or-other. He falls in step beside me, a package tucked under his arm.

"Hiya, Bishop." He opens.

"Marco." I return the greeting.

"Got a gift for you from Mr. Santos."

He offers me the package while keeping his eyes ahead.

"He wishes you a full and speedy recovery."

I take the box and give it a quick glance. It's an expensive bottle of Drake's Single Malt. I smile. So I was right.

"Give Santos my regards and thanks for the hooch."

"See you 'round Bishop." He says and keeps walking past my office as I turn to head inside.

Portia is at her desk as I walk in and set the box down in front of her.

She cocks an eyebrow, "What's this?" she asks.

"Confirmation that Santos wasn't involved."

"So where does that leave us?"

"Back to wondering who Morelli used to sick his dogs on me."

I nod at her datatype. "What are you working on?"

"I was poking around trying to see what I could dig up on Mr. Rossi. You know, Sharespace and such."

"Anything?" I ask.

"Nothing. Guy doesn't exist on any social media."

I grunt and hobble into my office settling into my worn leather chair. I open Santos's gift and pour a generous helping. My fingers drum against the desk as I sift through the files Lt. Ryan sent over.

As I scroll through Benny "The Brick" Rossi's record, it hits me like a flash in the dark. Rossi hasn't been charged with a single crime in the past two years. *Not one.* That's not just a coincidence; that's damned near impossible, a huge red flag waving right in my face.

I lean back, letting the realization sink in. Two years of clean records? In this line of work, that doesn't just happen. Rossi's been flying under the radar, and there's only one explanation I can think of: he's turned informant.

A surge of adrenaline courses through me as pieces of the puzzle start to fall into place. Rossi, working as muscle for whoever pays him, but also feeding information back to the cops.

I reach for my phone, dialing Ryan's desk directly.

"Tom? Bishop. Listen, I was wondering if you could stop by my shop this afternoon. I may have something. No, not on the phone. Yeah. Okay. See you then."

People are rarely as smart as they think they are. Morelli thinks himself smart. Maybe he is, I don't know. What I do know is that he is confident. He's confident because he's been ruthless enough for long enough to become wealthy and powerful. He's got the D.A. and several judges in his pocket. He's confident that if he just stays out of sight for a while, the Police investigation into the bombing of my office will just go away. He's probably right. Me? I don't know if I'm all that smart, but I do know I'm patient. Maybe stubborn is a better word.

Morelli didn't have me roughed up out of any sort of love for his idiot nephew. He did it out of fear. Fear that I would pry a lead on his whereabouts out of Billy. It also means that wherever he is, Morelli is still tuned in to what's happening in the city. This thought adds another question to the puzzle, "How?"

The answer is pretty obvious. He's got someone inside the police department, of course. Not exactly a shocking revelation, but it's another piece of the puzzle. Whoever was running Rossi as a C.I. was the one. Had to be.

The shadows have grown longer when Lt. Ryan shuffles into my office, the worn floorboards protesting under his bulk. He nods a hello to Portia as I lead him into my inner sanctum. I motion for him to take a seat as I pour us both a shot of the Drake's. He takes an appreciative pull and coughs.

"That's the good stuff, Bishop." he says, appreciatively. "Now, what's so important that we couldn't talk on the phone. Not that I mind the hooch."

"Morelli's got someone inside your precinct." I explain my findings to him. "Whoever is running Rossi is your boy. Find out who that is and take a peek at his bank records, and you'll have him."

"*Sonofabitch*!" he breathes out.

He reaches for the bottle and pours himself another measure.

"Bishop, I swear . . . it's like living in a house where everywhere you look, you find more rot. Yeah, I'll run it. I'll smoke the bastard out."

"When you find out . . ." I offer.

"Yeah. I'll get you the name." He agrees.

"Hell Bishop, how do you know *I'm* not the one working for Morelli?"

"You're kidding right? No one on the take would dress as badly as you."

He laughs, "Screw you, Bishop." He stands, stubs out his smoke and makes his exit.

I walk out to Portia's desk.

"Anything else popping right now Ms. Vance?" I ask.

"All's quiet, Mr. Bishop," she replies.

"Let's pack it in for the night."

I turn for the door, then stop.

"Do me a favor, will ya? Gimme a call to let me know you made it home. I don't expect any trouble, but things are getting a bit tense."

She smiles warmly. "I will. You be careful too!"

I lay awake, listening to the sounds of the city carried in on a cool morning breeze. Gradually, I become aware that nothing hurts. Strange thing to take notice of, even stranger to be so glad of it. Sitting up in the bed, I stretch my back, relishing the experience. I look over at Potluck who is doing his own yawning and stretching routine.

"Gonna be a good day." I tell him. He cocks his head quizzically at me as I make my way to the kitchen. I feed Potluck and start the coffee before heading to the bathroom. I don't get premonitions. I don't think such things are really possible, but there was an air of expectancy fluttering around the edges of my thoughts. By the time I slide on my shoes, I'm actually eager to get to the office. I have no idea why.

A sense of urgency however, won't make time move any faster, and it's far too early to be in the office. I head to Bailey's for breakfast, only discovering that I'm actually hungry when the smells hit me. Ms. Betty, a cigarette hanging from her wrinkled lips, gives me a grunt of acknowledgment and sets down a cup of coffee. I order my usual and she gives me another grunt before heading off to the kitchen.

One of my ex-girlfriends, Brenda I think, once asked me why I liked this place so much. I remember not being able to give her a satisfactory answer. Only that some things just feel right. Like a well broken in pair of shoes or a comfortable chair. She didn't get it. Probably one of the reasons we broke up.

By the time I finish breakfast and my crossword, the sun has finally risen. I pay the shot and leave Ms. Betty a healthy tip. Potluck wags his nub in appreciation of the bacon I saved for him as I head down Terrace Street. The traffic has picked up a bit. People in a hurry to get to places they'd rather not be.

The sun glints off of Portia's sleek roadster as I park out front. Potluck waddles contentedly beside me as I enter the office.

"Good Morning, Mr. Bishop." Portia greets without looking up from her Datatype. "The Bail check came in for Scarpa."

"Well there's some good news." I allow, heading into the file room to grab some coffee.

I pour a healthy cup and grab a seat opposite her desk.

"Anything else?"

Wordlessly, she slides over a small stack of phone messages.

"Nothing earth-shaking," I mumble rifling through the messages.

Two prospective clients. I'll call them back. A message from the garage that my car is due in for a tune up, and a message that some dry cleaning I'd forgotten was ready for pickup . . . the exciting life of a private detective.

As I light a smoke, my eyes suddenly take in new additions to the office. There's a rug under my feet now, and ferns and other plants tastefully placed about the room and curtains over the blinds behind her desk.

"Spruced up a bit?" I ask.

"The place needed a woman's touch. I hope it doesn't foul up your *nouveau-poverty* aesthetic."

I chuckle and head into my own office. I hang my hat and coat on the back of the door and plunk down behind my desk. I quickly get lost in scouring through the day's news and my own D-mails. Ellington's "I Got it Bad" croons softly from the radio, lulling me into a warm lassitude.

My eyes drift over the headlines—politics, crime, society's usual woes. A robbery on the north side, a missing socialite, another politician caught with his hand in the cookie jar.

The D-mails have piled up, a digital mountain of messages and memos, each one demanding a slice of my time. I sift through them mechanically, but my mind is elsewhere. Nothing important. The rhythm of the music sways with the ticking of the old clock on my wall, each second stretching out longer than the last. I lean back, the chair groaning under my weight, and let my gaze drift to the window. I rub my temples and glance at the clock. I've burned through half a pack of smokes and time has slipped by, unnoticed, stolen by the music.

A knock on the door jolts me back to the present. I blink, shaking off the trance, and straighten up.

"Jake?" Portia asks, hesitantly.

"What is it?"

"The device cracked open Morelli's accounts."

"Finally!" I rise from my chair and follow her back to her desk.

She scrolls through the multiple accounts, shaking her head.

"Regular deposits across all of them, but not a single withdrawal. I'm sorry, Jake."

I give her a smile.

"That's exactly what I needed."

"What? There's nothing here."

"The *nothing* tells me everything!"

I jog back to my office, grabbing my hat and coat.

"I need to borrow your car."

"What for?" she asks, tossing me her keys.

"I need to be conspicuous. Back soon!" And with that, I head out, leaving a very confused secretary behind.

I curse myself for an idiot as I wind my way through the downtown traffic. Money. It's always about the money! There was no movement in Morelli's official banking records, but there was absolutely no chance he was living low. Not Morelli. No, wherever he had planted himself, he would be living in luxury. That means money. When the mob moved finances off the books, they did it through *shadow bankers*.

There was one such individual used by the Italians, the Irish, the Russians, and God knows who else. Whitey Doyle. If you needed money moved off the books, Doyle was your man. He operated out of a legitimate pawnshop in the business district of Irongate. Doyle's was the place to go if you were a whisper away from ruin. Where the last shreds of dignity could be pawned for a breath of borrowed time.

I park around the corner and wait. For this to work, I have to be sure that Morelli still has some of his boys keeping an eye on me. I smoke a cigarette before finally getting out of the car. I walk past the pizza place and the liquor store before entering the innocuous storefront. Two suits stand opposite, in the shade of an awning over the entrance to a shoe store. Good.

Inside, the shelves are filled with radios, datatypes, electronics and collectibles. The walls hold rows of musical instruments. A glass counter encases glittering ranks of gold and silver rings, each of them a testimony to heartbreaks and breakups. Behind the glass counter were racks of rifles and pistols and a four-foot-tall Delores.

"Well well. Jake Bishop! How the hell are you, boy?" If asphalt could talk, it would sound like Delores. She was Whitey's sole employee, and the only muscle the place had ever needed.

Her face, wrinkled and tanned, is adorned by too much makeup in a vain attempt at preserving a youth long departed. Her hot pink blouse and skirt, pearls and pumps, ridiculous on anyone else, are perfectly natural to her.

"Hiya, Delores. Is he in?" I smile in spite of myself.

Delores "Dotty" Whipple had sent more than one shoplifter or troublemaker to the hospital with lead in him.

"Yeah, he's in the back, balancing the books." She wags a skeletal, nicotine-stained finger at me. "But don't you be causin' no trouble, Jake Bishop!"

"Relax Delores. I'm not here for trouble. Just talk."

She casts a gimlet eye and pushes a button under the counter. There's a buzzing sound and the door, marked "PRIVATE", pops open.

"Thanks Doll, I know the way."

Aged floorboards creak under my feet as I pass row after row of shelves piled high with pawned goods. The place smells old and musty. The only light streams in through windows high on the wall to my right, the beams dancing through the perpetual dust.

Doyle's private office is as luxurious as decades of hoarding the forfeited collectibles of the desperate could provide. An opulent space more suited to Beacon Hill than a downtown pawnshop, it's a decadence of comfort. Doyle got his nickname, "Whitey" for his thick coif of snow white wavy hair, and his Hollywood tan and movie star mustache.

"Hello, Doyle," I greet plopping down into one of the thickly padded maroon leather chairs opposite his over-sized mahogany desk.

He closes the topside datatype and ledger he'd been working on and leans back in mild surprise.

"Jake Bishop." He returns the greeting, with thinly veiled disdain. "How can I help you?"

"Wanted to talk a little business." I reply.

"Unless you're looking to pawn that ridiculous fedora, we have no business." He smiles, lighting a thin cigar with a jeweled lighter.

"I like my hat."

"Of course. Forgive my sarcasm. How can I help you?" he repeats.

"Well Doyle, it's like this: I'm hunting Morelli . . . he's gone to ground somewhere. Having a helluva time getting a bead on him too. I did some checking and he's not moving any money out of his personal accounts."

I lean forward with my elbows on his desk, fixing him with my stare.

"We both know he ain't holed up in some road-side shit hole, so that means he's getting funds."

I reach over and use Doyle's expensive lighter on my cheap cigarette. There's some discount philosophy for you.

"What makes you think I know anything about that?" he bluffs, coolly.

"Don't play dumb Doyle. Everyone knows you're the cookie pusher for the outfit. What you're going to tell me is, *where* you're sending the funds."

"Now you're the one being foolish if you think I would help you." He retorts. "Any possible dealings I might have with any alleged clients are confidential."

"Geez, Doyle, less than five minutes with you and I already feel like pasting you a few just to take the edge off a lousy afternoon."

I begin to rise.

Whitey recoils in his chair at the same moment I hear the hammer being pulled back on a pistol.

"Don't you lay a finger on him." Delores says from the doorway, a huge .45 in her tiny hand. "I told you no rough stuff!"

I sit back down and smile.

"You're right Delores. There's no need to get messy."

Doyle relaxes somewhat as I flick ashes on his expensive rug.

"So here's what's gonna happen. You're gonna tell me what I want to know, and I'll walk out of here looking frustrated, or you'll keep quiet and I'll walk out of here celebrating."

"What?" he breathes.

"You see, two of Morelli's boys watched me come in here. They'll know what we talked about. If you hold out on me, well . . . I'll just let the street choir sing any song they like about our little meeting. Not my fault if they get the wrong idea. What the outfit thinks about a rat holding their money is none of my business."

It's Delores who responds. "Bishop, that's just plain mean!"

"So's having your friends blown up." I reply, hotter than I intended.

It has the desired effect. Delores uncocks her heater and lowers it.

"You know we had nothing to do with any of that ugliness." Doyle offers.

"No, but your client did. I'm going to get him, one way or the other Doyle. How you come out in it all is entirely up to you."

"Damn you, Bishop!"

Back on the sidewalk, I pretend to call my office, lamenting that it was another dead end. I scowl and angrily walk back to my car, hiding my smile of satisfaction. Once I was actually driving, I make a real call.

"Portia? How do you feel about a trip to Eden Cove?" I chuckle at her enthusiasm.

"Yeah, it's a helluva drive. I'll pick you up and we'll stop at your place so you can pack. Yeah, a few days I think. Right. See you in a few."

# ACT 3: EDEN COVE

The afternoon sun is oppressively bright as I park outside the office.

"Excuse me Mr. Bishop." A deep baritone calls softly.

There's an unwritten rule in the underworld: You leave the bankers alone. Messing with the money men was forbidden. There are always consequences. Cause and effect. Doyle had wasted no time making the call, summoning an enforcer to settle the score. In this case, it was "Gentleman" Jack Brady, a freelancer with the Irish outfit, who was sent to make the books balance. The devil would have his due, and the devil had sent his big brother.

"I wonder if I might have a word with you." He rumbles.

Brady was easily seven feet tall and pushing three hundred pounds of muscle. His rolled pin-stripe shirtsleeves reveal forearms that ripple beneath red hair like steel cables. A derby set low over his eyes shades most of his face, save an over-sized mustache under a bulbous nose.

A slice of rotten luck big enough to choke on. I'd hoped to be well on my way before the wrath of Whitey Doyle caught up to me. Dammit.

"Can it wait, Brady? I'm in a bit of a hurry," I counter, guardedly.

"I really must insist," he growls.

The world turns upside down as I am lifted off my feet and hurled . . . hurled! . . . a dozen feet through the air into the alley. The trashcans scatter as I crash into them. Before I can gather my wits, Brady is on me. I don't know how long it lasts, but I am seeing stars and spitting blood as I gasp for breath. As I try to regain my feet, Brady speaks calmly over his shoulder, walking away, "Apologies for the discomfort, Mr. Bishop.

I'll assume we won't need to talk again. Have a nice day."

Brady had made his point, and I couldn't deny that I'd crossed a line by threatening Doyle. But in this game, you don't get far without breaking a few rules, even if it means paying for it in blood.

I manage to plant myself on my rump, leaning against the bare brick wall. Reaching shakily into my coat pocket, I pull out my phone and call inside.

"Portia? I'm outside. Yeah. Bring your stuff and Potluck. Oh, and bring the first aid kit will ya?" I don't remember ending the call. I must have blacked out for a minute there.

The highway stretches endlessly ahead, the sun gradually receding to the right. I fill Portia in on what I'd gotten from Doyle, explaining why I'd gotten tuned up by Brady. Portia stares out the window, the ebbing light accentuating her lovely features, focused on something I cannot read.

"That was a helluva chance to take." She turns back to me. "These guys are murderers, Jake. You won't avenge anyone if you die."

"Killing me would have brought too much heat on Doyle, he ain't that stupid. Besides, I'm not that easy to kill." She looks at me with doubtful eyes.

"So how does all this work exactly?" She asks.

"Morelli has a bolt hole account. They call it 'go-to-Hell' money.  Fake name, fake identity. That's why there was no movement in Morelli's accounts that we could see. Doyle set the whole thing up years ago."

"So the account has an address attached to it?"

"Yeah, but I got a dollar that says it goes to a drop. There's still some gum-shoeing left to do."

"We'll hit Eden Cove late," I say, breaking the stillness.

"Too late to really accomplish anything. Book us in someplace will ya."

Portia nods, her fingers tapping swiftly on her datatype. "Any preferences?"

"Someplace that won't turn me into a pauper," I smirk.

Portia taps a few keys on her datatype.

"All set. We're booked into a place called 'The Four Winds.' It's about the last thing available. I managed to snag fairly affordable accommodations."

I grunt an affirmation, wondering what *fairly affordable* would run me as we ride on in silence, the big v-8 purring smoothly through the late afternoon. The rolling hills gradually transform into gentle slopes, with forests of hardwoods sliding past on both sides of the road.

As the shadows grow longer and the sun begins to fade, we stop for gas and food in a little place that only exists because the railroad used to make a stop there. Soon after, Portia is dozing beside me as I wash down the last of the now stale coffee. The air is fresh and clean blowing through the open windows as we snake our way ever southward. After all this time, I'm finally going to get the bastard. That thought, more than the smokes and coffee, keeps me awake and alert as we wind our way through the picturesque countryside.

There's a tang of salt air wafting in on the breeze, and the full moon hangs heavy in the sky as I finally make the last turn into Eden Cove. The birches and elms have long since given way to palmettos, palms, and live oaks with heavy beards of Spanish moss.

I give Portia a gentle shake. "We're here."

She stretches sensually and gives a demure yawn. "What time is it?"

"Almost eleven. Pull up directions to the hotel, will ya?"

We make a few twists and turns and arrive at the hotel. At first, the place strikes me as far too opulent for my paltry budget. Then I realize every place we'd passed in this resort town was equally lavish, even the gas stations. So this is how the other half lives.

When we enter the lobby, I'm flattened by fatigue, so Portia confidently takes the lead. We're greeted by a diminutive dandy in hotel livery.

"Hello," he breathes haughtily. "Welcome to the Four Winds."

"Reservation for Mr. and Mrs. Pembroke?" Portia says.

I raise an eyebrow.

"Ah yes, the Honeymoon Suite! Welcome! I'm David, your concierge. Should you need anything, please don't hesitate to call on me."

Honeymoon suite? Sheesh.

He hands Portia his card and snaps his fingers.

"James here will show you to your room."

A young kid, no more than 17, takes our bags enthusiastically.

"Right this way, folks!" Portia hooks her arm in mine, playing her part to the hilt.

James leads us down a broad corridor through deep piled carpet to an ornate door.

"Here we are," he says, unlocking the door.

"Darling, aren't you going to carry me across the threshold?" Portia asks, raising an eyebrow at me.

I walk past her into the spacious suite, "My back hurts, honey." I slide the kid a twenty and close the door behind him.

Portia wraps her arms around my neck, standing on her tiptoes, and gives me a playful kiss. "Alone at last," she quips. I spin her around and give her rump a slap.

"Pour me a scotch, wife!" She giggles and trots over to the en suite bar, pouring each of us a generous slug.

I take off my hat and coat, hanging them on the provided hall tree. I walk out to the balcony, overlooking the beach. Yes, this would do just fine! Portia joins me, leaning over the railing, taking it all in. The stars are beautiful, and the waves gently caressing the shore whisper comfortingly.

"Never been to the beach before," she offers. "Pictures . . . movies . . . they don't do it justice!"

I grunt an agreement and head back inside, kicking off my shoes. Portia takes her bag and disappears into the restroom. I'm stripping off my shirt and tie when the obvious slaps me in the face.

"Portia," I call out. "There's only one bed. Guess I'll take the sofa."

She emerges from the bathroom wearing only a sheer nightie, pads over to me, and pulls my head down to hers. She kisses me deeply and breathes, "No, I don't think that'll be necessary." I give in this time and return her kiss. I don't know why I ever resisted in the first place.

The night is hot, steamy, and passionate. The rest is none of your business.

Room service provides a complimentary breakfast, which we take on the balcony. Portia nibbles on bacon, alternately sipping her coffee and orange juice. I scan the nearby beach houses with my binoculars.

"No way of knowing which it might be." I grumble, putting down the binoculars and pouring a fresh cup of coffee. I'm disgusted with myself for not thinking of how many such places existed. *Dammit*! I'd been so excited about closing in on the bastard, that I'd forgotten how much more work was still to be done.

"You'll think of something, I'm sure." Portia reassures, rising from the table and giving me a grin. "I'm going to shower while you do your detective thing!"

*My detective thing. Sure, why didn't I think of that*?! But, I *am* a detective! I *can* do detective stuff!

I re-enter the room, sit on the bed and grab the phone-book, looking up seasonal rentals. "Low-country Rentals" is the first one I see. An eager, friendly *Madge* takes my call.

"Here's the thing," I lie, "My wife and I are honeymooning here and she really loves it. I'm thinking we might want to rent a more long term place, stay for the whole season. A nice beach house, maybe."

I give the agent time to pour out the usual sales pitches.

"Wonderful," I continue. "Sure, we can come by. Okay, thank you!"

Portia emerges from the bathroom, wrapped in a towel and a cloud of steam. I explain my idea and the part I want her to play.

"See, that's some damn fine detective-ing, Jake Bishop!" She drops her towel with a teasing grin to get dressed, and I take in the view.

In due course, we pull into the rental agency, looking every bit the tourist honeymooners. Madge greets us enthusiastically, leading us into her quaint office. The walls are sea green and beige, overdone with nautical accents like drift-wood and shells. Large windows draped in bil-lowy white curtains let in natural light, and a gen-tle breeze. Her desk is loaded with brochures and beachfront property listings. Wicker chairs with blue cushions encircle a coffee table adorned with seashells, as if a visitor needed reminding that they were on the coast.

Her southern charm is lost on me, smacking instead of enthusiastic greed. Good. I like greedy people. Makes them easy to manipulate.

Madge provides us with coffee, information about the amenities the city provides, brochures, chit chat, and a list of available properties. We make all the right noises and, right on cue, Portia turns to me.

"Oh darling, can we go and see some of these?"

"I don't see why not. That is, if Madge here has the time." I give the agent an imploring look.

"Certainly!" She claps her hands. "Just let me get my keys!"

We're walking toward Madge's car when I wince and double over, holding my side.

"Oh Darling, is it your gall bladder again?" Portia puts a supportive arm around me, her voice oozing concern. I nod my head, continuing the theatrics.

"What can I do?" Madge offers helpfully.

"I'm okay," I say. "It happens sometimes. I just need to take my medicine and lay down."

I rise up and lean against the car.

"Honey, you go ahead and look. I'll meet you back at the resort."

"Are you sure, darling?" Portia asks.

"We can reschedule, if you need to." Madge offers.

"No. It's okay. You two go on ahead. If she finds something she likes, I'll come back and give it a look."

I don't wait for agreement. I give Portia a gentle kiss, fish out my own keys and head for my own car.

"Okay, Darling." Portia calls. "I'll see you back at the resort."

I see them out of the corner of my eye getting into Madge's car, hushed tones of concern wafting over the distant waves. I pull out behind them, turning in the direction opposite of theirs. I navigate the sparse traffic, looking for a convenient spot, finally parking behind a nearby pharmacy. I allow time for Madge to be well away and open a shadowgate, emerging in the lobby we had just vacated.

Inside, I make my way to the back. Madge's files contain the listings of the properties she personally manages. The files have copies of the lease, payment schedules and receipts. Nothing in those look interesting. I go to her datatype and open a master file, containing all the rental and lease properties in Eden Cove. I filter by oc-

cupancy status and date. Gotcha! Ten months
ago, a long term beach house was leased to one
"Vincent Marconi."

I shake my head as I print the file. Some people just lack imagination! Vincent Marconi/Vito
Morelli. I find the street address on the map
Madge had so helpfully provided. Perfect. *I've
got you now, you punk!* I shadowstep back to my
car, immediately regretting not having rolled the
window down. The heat in the black interior takes
my breath away. I crank up the air conditioning
and drive back to the resort, smiling in spite of
the heat.

It's late afternoon when Portia returns. She
drops her purse on the dresser and sighs, lighting
a cigarette.

"That woman never shuts up!" She breathes
out, exasperated. "I swear, she could sell water
to the fish!"

She walks over to where I'm sitting, with a map splayed out in front of me and leans over.

"You found him." she whispers.

"Bet your bloomers, Doll." I give her a smile.

"Tomorrow morning, you and I are gonna spend the day beach-combing." She returns the smile, her eyes alight with anticipation. "In the meantime, let's go see what we can find for dinner."

We decide against the upscale seafood eateries that populate the tourist areas like crows in a cornfield. The trick to finding good places to eat or drink in resort towns is to find a place with local license plates in the parking lot. The locals know where the good stuff is. We settle on a quiet mom and pop place that does simple fare.

Red vinyl booths line the walls, their seats cracked and well-worn but still inviting. Each booth features a small tabletop jukebox, where a coin buys you a selection from the top hits.

A counter stretches along the right side, with chrome stools topped with red vinyl cushions beneath. Behind the counter, shelves display glass jars filled with colorful candies and a showcase of homemade pies: apple, cherry, and lemon meringue.

Ceiling fans stir the cool air, carrying the faint scent of roasted coffee beans and sizzling hamburgers. Waitresses in pastel uniforms with white aprons bustle between tables, balancing trays loaded with hearty meals and milkshakes. The clink of plates and the murmur of conversation create a comforting buzz.

Portia and I find a booth towards the back, away from the other scattered patrons. She orders a cheeseburger and fries, I opt for the corned beef special.

"Jake," Portia asks between bites. "I hesitate to ask, but what exactly are you going to do with Morelli when you get to him?"

"What do you mean?" I ask. "I'm gonna call the locals to make the arrest and then get Tom Ryan to come down and serve the extradition warrant."

"No," she replies. "I mean, what if he resists? What if he tries to kill you or have one of his men do it?" She whispers, casting a cautious glance toward the other patrons.

"I can handle it." I give her a reassuring smile. "I just gotta be sure to catch him off guard. I can't give him a chance to run. I may never catch up to him again."

"And if he's got the Judge and District Attorney on the hook, won't all of this be for nothing?"

"If all of this was just to get him on front of the local judge, you'd be right, but the Feds are stepping in. The FBI has its own case running because Morelli's crimes cross state lines and involve organized crime. By bringing federal charges and moving the case to federal court, we're bypassing the local system entirely."

Portia nods thoughtfully, her inner thoughts hidden behind sky blue eyes. I can tell my answer didn't really satisfy her concerns, but she's polite enough to let it drop.

Truth be told, I'm worried about how far the corruption has spread also, but that's not really for me to address. All I can do is play the cards I'm dealt. I'll nab the bastard and let Ryan get him to the feds. After that, it's outta my hands.

Standing to leave, I drop a heavy tip and take Portia's arm. We pile into the car and head back to the Four Winds, contented and quiet.

Conveniently, Morelli's beach house is not that far from our place. We dress the part of beach-combers, me in khakis and a loud Hawaiian shirt, Portia in a wispy sundress and hat. We chuff through the thick sand and the gentle surf, paus-ing from time to time to take pictures. When we get to a spot close to our quarry, I pose Portia in front of the place and use the zoom lens to do a quick reconnaissance. We spread a blanket and set out our picnic lunch. Just a couple of honeymooners enjoying the beach.

I uncork a bottle of champagne and pour for each of us. The sound of the surf and breeze covers our conversation. I'm careful not to stare.

"This is gonna be harder than I thought." I confess.

Portia raises a quizzical eyebrow as she puts together a couple of sandwiches.

"There's three outside the place. Two on the veranda, one down on the lawn. Gotta be at least that many around the back and two or three more inside. Place is lousy with muscle."

"Are you saying you can't get him?" She asks with an anxious look.

I shake my head, chewing the ham and cheese, chasing it with the bubbly.

"No, I'll get him, just gonna have to get creative."

"Can't you just do your teleport thing?" She asks.

"Doesn't work like that. I've either gotta know the place I'm going, or be able to see it," I explain.

We eat in silence while I think about how to deal with the situation.

Portia surprises me by asking, "Jake, would a distraction help get you inside?"

"What are you thinking?" I ask.

I don't like the idea of using her for any part of the takedown. In answer, she stands up and grabs the basket.

"I've got just the thing. C'mon!" she says.

I grab the blanket and the rest of our gear. She takes my arm, leaning against my shoulder and guides us back toward our suite.

Back in our room, Portia ducks into the restroom. I change out of my beach wear and into my normal clothing. I don't anticipate anything going wrong, but the last thing I'd want is to be killed wearing a Hawaiian shirt! I pour a shot of liquid fortitude and step out onto the balcony. The weight of what we're about to do settles heavily on my shoulders.

"Well, what do you think?" Portia asks from behind me.

I turn and my heart skips a beat. She's wearing a tiny yellow bikini that leaves nothing to the imagination. She turns around playfully, giving me a complete view.

"What do I think?" I laugh, "I think you're a distraction alright. Hell, you may just get yourself arrested!"

She takes the scotch from my hand with a mischievous smile and takes a sip. We both sit at the little bistro table on the balcony.

"I'll wear a wrap until we get started, Jake. I'm not looking to get arrested." She gives a giggle, "Are you suggesting I'm indecent?"

I decide I'm done letting her catch me on the short hop and retort, "I'm not suggesting anything. You *are* totally and completely indecent, Ms. Vance." I light us each a smoke. "Seriously though, I don't want you getting hurt. Some of these guys are real animals," I say, unable to keep the worry from my voice.

"I'll be fine, Jake." She counters, "Besides, if this is going to happen, you're gonna need a distraction."

We spend some time working out the details, refining things as much as possible. I want us to move at sunset, when the light and shadows do funny things to vision and when people start to relax. The east facing beach house's spacious porch will be in shadow at that time. For this to work, I need every edge I can get.

"That's a lot of time to kill," Portia says, rising from the table and walking toward the French doors.

She looks back at me over her shoulder. "Whatever shall we do to occupy ourselves?" She unties her top, lets it fall to her feet, and walks into the suite.

Who am I to argue?

I find a good spot behind some shrubs in the neighboring lawn. I can see most of Morelli's veranda, and have eyes on the three goons out front. A few lights are on downstairs, toward the back. In due course, Portia comes into view, walking casually. Even from here, the sun glinting on her curves draws the eye. She stops just short of the path leading up to Morelli's, opens her little bag, and fishes out a cigarette. She makes a theatrical display of not being able to strike her lighter. She stomps her foot in exasperation and looking up, seems to just notice the men out front.

"Say boys," she calls out to them. "What's a girl gotta do to get a light?" The one on the lawn reaches in his pocket and heads her way. The two on the porch give each other a look, and then they too trot down the stairs. Yes!

As they crowd around her, I make my move. Sticking to the lengthening shadows, I quickly and quietly scale the steps. I turn left at the top and give a quick peek inside. The foyer is dark and empty. There's no sign of activity.

Chances are, the boys inside will be keeping their eyes on the doors and maybe the windows. I don't need either. I focus my power and smoothly pass through the wall into the foyer. Inside, I stand perfectly still, commanding my heart to slow down. I listen intently for a full minute. Somewhere in the back, a radio plays. The faint smell of cigarette smoke lingers in the air. I edge down the short hallway and carefully look around the corner.

Morelli is there, sitting in a comfortable arm-chair, smoking a thick cigar. One of his men, slightly closer to me, is also smoking, leaning indolently against the wall. Another is perched on a stool to my left, reading a magazine. Both goons are armed, their pistols tucked into shoulder holsters.

Again, I draw on my power and lay on a glamour. Into it, I pour the months of pain, the guilt, and the anguish since the bombing. For Frank and for Mary, funerals for friends I could not attend, friends I would never see again! I silently step into the room, letting the horror radiate from me.

"Morelli." I growl from behind clenched teeth. The guards momentarily recoil from the glamour, but one of them, to his credit, goes for his gun. I gesture and it simply breaks into a dozen pieces, raining down on the hardwood floor at his feet. He looks at his empty hand, befuddled. I step closer to him and give him a hard kick in the gut. He doubles over as his partner comes charging toward me.

I sidestep his clumsy punch, countering with a straight right to his jaw. He goes down hard on his knees fumbling for his gun. I repeat the disassembly trick and kick him squarely in the face. Both men are down and appear to be out of the fight. I turn to face Morelli, a grim smile on my face.

"You went through my boys pretty quick-like, Bishop. Impressive, I'll give you that." he begins, rising from his chair and stepping toward me.

"But what do you think you're gonna accomplish? I'm Vito Morelli! I *own* Solomon City! I *own* the cops! I *own* the judges, I *own* the D.A.! You think a two bit, gumshoe like you is gonna be the one to bring me down?! You're a bigger idiot than I thought. I'll never set foot in court!"

"I'm the one taking you in, Morelli, not your corrupt cops. And I won't be handing you over to the system you've bought and paid for. The Feds are in this now, and you don't own them!"

"Ha! Is that what you think? I've got more politicians working for me than you've got hairs on your head, punk! Your best bet is to get outta my sight while you can! Ain't a court in the land that will try me!" He threatens.

"He's right, Jake." a voice calls from behind me. I turn and see Portia standing behind me, a snub-nosed .38 in her hand, pointed at Morelli.

"You?!" Morelli gasps.

"Yes, you bastard, me!" She cocks the pistol.

"Portia, no!" I shout and lunge toward her. Too late. The pistol fires, striking Morelli above his left eye. He falls like an empty suit to the cold floor, in a puddle of his own blood.

"I'm sorry, Jake, but he had to die." She drops the pistol and slumps into a chair, her head in her hands.

The stars are out and the night is warm and crisp. Lt. Ryan stands next to me in silence, puffing the stub of a cigar. A crowd of onlookers stands behind the yellow crime scene tape, as Morelli's lifeless body is rolled into the back of the coroner's van. I light a cigarette and watch from the porch as a female detective loads Portia into the back of a police car. Our eyes meet and she shows me her dimples one last time.

Turns out, Morelli had been responsible for the death of Portia's fiancé. Seems he'd been a bright young journalist who was digging into organized crime in Solomon City. He'd gotten too close to Morelli's outfit and had gotten himself gunned down outside of a movie theater, right in front of Portia.

She'd used me as a stalking horse. She'd read about my case in the papers, and had answered my ad for a secretary, hoping I would get to him where the police had failed. It all made sense now. Her determination and eagerness to find Morelli. Working the long hours for such little pay. I shoulda checked her background myself, but I'd fallen for her good looks and keen abilities. Serves me right.

So now, Morelli escapes the chair and Portia Vance is facing life. I shake my head and step on my cigarette, snuffing it out.

A damned dirty thing.

# About the Author

Christopher "Doc" Blalock is a US Navy veteran Corpsman and retired counselor. He is a prolific fine artist, illustrator, musician, sculptor and writer, cursed with the itch to create. He draws inspiration from sources ranging from JRR Tolkien to Tom Clancy. He additionally draws from his love of classic black-and-white noir films, infusing their moody aesthetic and storytelling into his writing. A helpless coffee addict, he lives in the Atlanta suburbs with his childhood sweetheart and a dog of dubious moral character.